SONGS

THAT CHANGED
OUR LIVES

BRUCE BURCH

EGGMAN • PUBLISHING

Editor:
  Isabel Anders

Cover Design by:
  Bill Tyler

Cover Photo by:
  Bill Thorup

Design, typography, and text production:
  TypeByte Graphix

Library of Congress: 95-61554

ISBN: 1-886371-25-3

Eggman Publishing
3012 Hedrick Street
Nashville, Tennessee 37203
(800) 396-4626

In Memory of

Kyle Lynch
Taylor Melinda Caldwell
Robert Leggett
Hank Williams, Sr.

&

In Honor of

Tony Moore
Robert Williams
Brooke Gall
Candy Winnett
Judy Shepherd
Buddy & Carlene Kalb
Patty Gallagher

Contents

Acknowledgments

I don't know whether to bless 'em or blame 'em (I'll let you, the reader, be the judge) — but I'd like to offer heartfelt (as well as head-aching) thanks to the following people:

Richard Courtney and *Eggman Publishing* for giving me the confidence to write this book, and also for doing a great job editing the bad grammar of a University of Georgia graduate.

Loretta, Loudilla, and *Kay Johnson* and the *International Fan Club Organization (IFCO)* for their help and support in this project. Also, much appreciation to all the fan club presidents across the country who, through their newsletters, helped solicit the stories used in this book. The response was tremendous!

BLT Management for their major contribution in making possible my first "literary work." Thanks for taking a gamble *Larry Lockamy!*

M. Shane Hamilton, my "psychic sidekick," for all the hours he contributed to this project — as well as for his commitment to its quality.

Robert Reynolds of **The Mavericks** for a wonderful foreword. And to *Steve Navyac* for his help in getting Robert to write the foreword.

Shannon McCombs for her enthusiasm in this project and the "Daddy's Hands" story.

Jenny Bohler for her assistance in the "Is There Life Out There" story.

Isabel Anders for the final editing of my (and Richard's) mistakes!

Allison Auerbach for all the information she provided.

Kim Blake and **Bruce Allen Management** for your encouragement and help with the "Independence Day" story.

Bill Tyler for the cover, and **Bill Thorup** for the cover photo.

All my friends who read the first draft and told me it was good (those of you who had no comment, thanks for not telling me it was bad).

All the people and their families who shared their sometimes painful stories with us for this book.

My family in Georgia for all their years of love.

Cindy, Sarah, and Matthew Burch — the greatest family anyone could ever hope for. Yours are "the lives that changed my life." I could never express how much you mean to me, but I hope you know. Also, **Nutmeg Burch,** our 17-year-old dog who passed away January 1, 1995 — we miss you, "Nutty"!

If there is anyone I left out, I'll buy you dinner . . . *IF* this book sells well.

A Special Word

This book is dedicated to three very special groups of people. First, to the songwriter. It is a difficult task to pour one's heart out onto a piece of paper and make the words rhyme and flow. The odds against getting a song recorded are astronomical. For a song to become a hit requires nothing short of a miracle.

Each day thousands of songs are written by thousands of songwriters willing to take up this task. Why? Not for the money. Very few songwriters ever make a dime. If you were to add up the years it took for them to finally be paid for writing a song, and to calculate the hourly wage they earned in pursuing this "career," it would probably amount to only a few cents an hour. Songwriters write songs because they have to. Emotions that cannot be locked inside must spill out. Every now and then these emotions are transformed into hit songs, their energies flowing through recording artists, stirring listeners. There is no greater joy for a songwriter than to hear his or her song on the radio, knowing that millions of people across the world are also listening. There is no bigger thrill for a songwriter than to be sitting at a concert when an artist performs one of his or her songs, and thousands of people sing along, knowing every word.

Perhaps this is the true reason that songwriters write songs—and the dream they chase. It is my hope that in some way this book pays tribute to that dream.

I would also like to dedicate this book to the recording artists who record the songs. They give the songwriters' dreams a voice. They are the vessels who carry the songs to the fans.

Most artists spend 250 to 300 days a year on the road, taking their music to their fans. There are some who play big concert halls and arenas. But the majority of country entertainers perform in small, dingy, smoky nightclubs and neon honky tonks. The glamor of show business is hard to find in the lives of these artists. They face a grueling series of one-nighters. They arrive in a new town every day, after traveling all night trying to sleep on a bumpy tour bus—in most cases with several other band members aboard. A moment in the spotlight usually takes the performer years to achieve.

The stories in this book (and there are thousands more out there) will let these great entertainers know that they are doing more than simply entertaining. Their music is truly a part of their fans' lives. And in many cases, it helps fans survive circumstances in their lives which otherwise they might not have been able to face.

Finally, this book was written to honor the country music fan. There are no fans more dedicated in any other genre of music. Perhaps it is because most country songs are inspired by the lives of average, everyday people that so many of them can identify with these songs. From the thousands of letters we received in researching this book, it is obvious that the lyrics of these songs are more than just pages of words that rhyme. People gather strength and solace in their time of need from the sad songs of love and loss. Their spirits are lifted by the uptempo dance numbers, and their hearts are warmed by the classic story songs.

The response of fans may be the greatest reason why the songwriter writes and the singer sings. For without the fans to listen, the song would be silent.

Thanks to all the country music fans who sent us the stories contained in this book, and to all who will read it.

I hope you see a little of your life in some of these songs and the stories they have inspired.

Bruce Burch–December, 1995

Foreword

Songs are the mirror image of life; they reflect perfectly the way we move and feel. In words and melody, our journey is charted by music.

It is through the gift of the songwriter we are able to look into this mirror, and in the reflection of song, we better understand our lives.

In *Songs That Changed Our Lives*, Bruce Burch has masterfully translated the power of music as it relates the journeys of eleven individuals.

When I was asked to write the foreword to this book, I anticipated more of the standard fare of boy meets girl, girl meets boy, they fall in love type. That is certainly not the case in this book. These stories relate to cases wherein music made drastic, positive, at times miraculous changes in the lives of people who really needed help in their lives. At times it is probably better that the songwriter is not aware of the depth of the mirror and weight that the words and melodies carry in the lives of others.

The power of music is, however, undeniably real, and through this book, the reader can begin to better understand and therefore better appreciate the work of the songwriters and recording artist who carry the power to the people.

Robert Reynolds, The Mavericks.

The First Verse

Music moves people. It touches them in ways no other art form can. A song has the ability to make the listener laugh, cry, perhaps think or dream — and it can even evoke love when it is least expected. A beautiful painting or sculpture in a museum of high art can stir emotions in someone, but the person must travel to an art exhibit to view it. A well-written novel or a piece of poetry can reach deep into its reader's soul, but still the book must be opened and the pages turned in order to be appreciated. An Oscar-winning film can bring tears or uncontrollable laughter, but there must be effort extended in order for the movie to be seen.

A song often sneaks up on its prey. The listener may be innocently driving along on a lonely back road or even a crowded interstate when a song leaps from the radio into the heart of its victim. There have been people who have literally had to pull off the road when they first heard a song, because they were unable to hold back their tears. People have written that they were in such despair that they were on the verge of taking their own lives — when a song reached them in a way that no therapist or friend ever could, and saved them.

There are countless others who connect a song to the exact moment that they fell in love. Every couple seems to have identified "their" song.

It is as if a Greater Power is the ultimate disc jockey, bringing songs and human beings together, perhaps at a time when they need to hear just that particular song.

Songs can change lives. I know, for about 20 years ago, mine was forever changed by one.

I had just suffered through my first year of college at a small Tennessee school which I had attended on a partial football scholarship. It was bad enough that my first taste of college football proved to be sour (our team went winless that year). To make matters worse, the distance from my hometown high-school sweetheart proved too great to keep our love alive. I lost her to my best friend back home!

Needless to say, I was one sad puppy that summer when I came home and she broke the news. I decided that football and college were not meant for me. I began drinking a great deal and lost sight of my goals. At that point, I simply did not care about anything. I was in Atlanta one summer weekend visiting a former teammate from my short-lived college football career. We happened by his sister's apartment one evening. When we walked in, I heard a Kris Kristofferson record playing. The song was *For the Good Times*. At that point in time, I was unfamiliar with Kris Kristofferson, nor had I ever listened to country music. The song hit me like a ton of bricks — actually more like a ton of concrete blocks! The words to that song conveyed what no one else had been able to say to me . . . not my family, not my friends, not even my high school sweetheart. . . .

Don't look so sad, I know it's over,
But life goes on, and this ole world will keep on turnin'.
Let's just be glad we had some time to spend together,
There's no need to watch the bridges that we're burnin'.

Lay your head upon my pillow,
Hold your warm and tender body close to mine
Hear the whisper of the raindrops blowin' soft against the window
And make believe you love me one more time
For the good times.

I'll get along, you'll find another
And I'll be here if you should find you ever need me
Don't say a word about tomorrow or forever,
There'll be time enough for sadness when you leave me.

Lay your head upon my pillow,
Hold your warm and tender body close to mine
Hear the whisper of the raindrops blowin' soft against the window
And make believe you love me one more time
For the good times.

While I was unable to hold my high-school sweetheart's *warm and tender body close to mine,* that song was the first step in being able to let her go.

And when I let her go, I picked up my brother's old guitar which had been left lying in a closet for several years after he had taken two or three guitar lessons and given up. I got a copy of that Kris Kristofferson record and the songbook containing the songs on the album. My fingers bled as I poured my heart into learning those songs. Soon I started writing songs of my own. And as I did, my life seemed to find direction again.

I made the decision to go back to school and transferred to the University of Georgia, from which I graduated in 1975. I tried teaching school and coaching football for a year, but I never stopped writing songs after I heard *For the Good Times.*

I moved to Nashville in 1976 to pursue a song-writing career. It took about 10 years of being a desk clerk, running a hot dog stand, waiting tables, and holding down several other less illustrious part-time and full-time jobs before I was able to make a living as a songwriter.

During the past 10 years, I have written two #1 songs recorded by Reba McEntire (*Rumor Has It* and *It's Your Call*), as well as several other top 40 records and multi-platinum album cuts.

The idea for this book is a result of many people approaching me and telling me how my songs, as well as the songs of others, have affected them. As I pondered their words, I realized how music had changed my life, and where it had led me.

As you read these stories about these great songs and the lives they have touched, I hope you will be as moved as I was. The stories come from people from all walks of life. It has been said that music knows no boundaries. It falls on any ear that is open and any heart that can hear. Let your heart hear these "Songs That Changed Our Lives."

Author's Note: We have asked the fans, whom the stories in this book are about, to list their favorite charities so readers might contribute in their names. These charitable organizations and their addresses are listed at the end of each chapter, in case you would like to donate to them.

The Dance

Garth Brooks

SONGWRITER:
Tony Arata

Lookin' back on the memory of
The dance we shared neath the stars above
For a moment all the world was right
How was I to know that you'd ever
    say goodbye

> *Chorus:*
> *And now I'm glad I didn't know*
> *The way it all would end*
> *The way it all would go*
> *Our lives are better left to chance*
> *I could have missed the pain*
> *But I'd of had to miss the dance*

Holding you I held everything
For a moment wasn't I a king
If I'd only known how the king would fall
Well then who's to say I might have changed
    it all

> *Repeat Chorus*

Our lives are better left to chance
I could have missed the pain
But I'd of had to miss the dance

In the past decade, country music has grown at a faster pace than ever before in its history. One of the greatest factors in, and primary reason for, this boom is a fellow named Garth Brooks.

Garth Brooks was a young man from Oklahoma who moved to Nashville in the mid-1980s, only to turn around and return home after a short stay. Though his first brush with breaking into the music business left him bruised, he refused to give up. When he moved to Nashville again with his wife Sandy in the late '80s, he came back to stay. Within a relatively short period of time, he secured a record deal with Capitol Records—and, as they say, the rest is history.

During his early days in Nashville in 1988, Garth met up with another newcomer to Music City. At a writer's night at the famous Bluebird Cafe, Garth shared the stage with another struggling writer named Tony Arata. It was on this night that Garth first heard Tony perform *The Dance*.

Tony and his wife, Jaymi, had moved to Nashville in 1987. Not long after their arrival, Tony wrote a beautiful melody. He tried and tried to write words to fit this melody. The first lyrics he wrote were completely different from the ones he ultimately settled on. When Tony was finally satisfied with the lyrics, the song ended up being titled *The Dance*. As Tony recalls:

"The lyrics that make up the song were inspired by a movie called *Peggy Sue Got Married*, which dealt with the issue of what could happen if you were given a chance to change the past, much like 'It's a Wonderful Life.' Both movies point out the fact that, even if you could go back in time, you don't get to pick and choose memories. If you change one thing, it affects everything else. So I chose one event, a dance, and tried to make the point that if this is the sweetest memory you have, then you have to take it along with the knowledge that you lost the one you loved and shared that dance with."

When Garth Brooks heard Tony perform *The Dance* that night at the Bluebird Cafe, he didn't hear it as a song about lost love. He heard it as a song about life or the loss of life. After their set was over, he told Tony that if he ever got a chance to make an album, he would love to record the song. Garth did not forget his promise; and when he recorded his first album, he included *The Dance*. It was chosen to be the fourth single off the album.

It proved to be huge on the radio; but what really made *The Dance* a classic was the video directed by John Lloyd Miller. He used Garth's vision of the song to turn the *The Dance* into a metaphor for life. The video opens with Garth explaining his interpretation of the song, mentioning the names of the people who appear in a collage of clips throughout the video. As Garth says: "These people that have given the ultimate sacrifice for a dream that they believed in—John F. Kennedy, Martin Luther King, John Wayne, and Keith Whitley . . . and if they could come back, I think they would say to us what the lyrics to *The Dance* say."

Clips of professional rodeo star Lane Frost, and footage of the astronauts killed in the Challenger explosion also appear in the video. The video, in the words of the song's writer, Tony Arata, "took the song to another level."

It also took Garth Brooks' career to another level. People across the world were drawn to this touching video, and it became one of the most popular in the history of the medium.

In Nashville, Tennessee, a young man named Kyle Lynch happened to walk through the room where his mother Karen was watching television. The video of *The Dance* was on, and though Kyle was not into country music, he stopped and watched it with his mother.

Kyle was a big fan of Jim Morrison and The Doors. Perhaps it was the poetic lyrics that initially caught his ear. As he and his mom watched, they both got tears in their eyes. And as the video ended, they talked about the message of the song: *I could have missed the pain, but I'd of had to miss the dance.*

Kyle, his mom Karen, and his sister Kari had been through their share of pain. When Kyle was 12 and Kari was nine, their father had walked out on the family in the middle of the night. Over the next few years, he had very little communication with his son and daughter, and in Karen's words, "offered no financial help."

Karen and her children moved in with her mother in Dallas, Texas, for a short period of time. Later, she was offered a job in Rock Hill, South Carolina, working for the gospel group, The Happy

Goodman Family. When the Goodman Family decided to move their home base to Nashville, Karen, Kyle, and Kari decided to go along.

Kyle became a freshman at Hillwood High School, and Karen was determined to settle down so that Kyle and Kari could both finish their remaining school years in one place. The family had finally arrived at a place where *for a moment, all the world was right.*

Kyle grew into a handsome young man, as well as a talented athlete. He especially excelled in football, and it became a big part of his life. Hillwood High School's football coach, Jerry Link, said this of Kyle: "He loved football. When he put his uniform on, you could see his eyes light up. We called him 'Hit Man' because he loved to hit people and wouldn't back down from anything. He was a good role model, and he gave the game everything he had."

His senior year, he made the most tackles on his team and was named Defensive Player of the Year. He loved the game so much, he intended to play college football at Austin Peay State University the following fall.

Kyle's "dance" was going extremely well. Perhaps this is why he identified with the Garth Brooks song in so many ways, and why it became one of his favorites. He and his family had overcome so much, and he must have felt *for a moment, wasn't I a king.* He was living life to its fullest and was filled with dreams. In fact, he co-wrote a poem about it with his friend Jerry Proenza.

Dreams

A lost young petal
Wondering souls
I see the dream you seek
Follow me please, if you dare.
The dream is coming
For you and me.
I return by your side
With a heart in my hand.
It is like a bright fire dancing
To the slow music turning.
My heart as smooth as ivory
Has turned to a lonely sulfur,
I retire my heart now to you,
Love me because I love you.

Still, a sense that *the king would fall* hung over Kyle. He was at a crossroads; and though he couldn't see what lay ahead, he must have had some premonition of *the way it all would end, the way it all would go.*

Karen was cooking supper one night when Kyle walked up and told her, "I've got the crazy feeling something is going to happen to me, and they are going to dedicate the annual to me." His mom told him not to ever think like that, and Kyle laughed in his usual laid-back way, saying, "Oh, Mom, it's just a crazy thought—nothing's gonna happen to me!"

Still the doubts troubled Kyle, as he wrote in this letter that was found tucked away in his room. It read:

This is to anyone. I'm writing because I need someone to talk to, someone to open myself to. I need to be held. Yes me. Even I am not made of brick, although I'm strong, even strong things break down at times.

Whoever reads, I don't want sympathy or talk, I just want someone to listen.

I sit here laid back, tears are falling from my face. I'm so scared. I feel so alone, so lost, confused, sad . . . I realize I'm not going to have all the things I love forever.

Starting off, friends. God, I've never felt this way. I look at their faces in my mind. What's going to happen? Will I ever see my friend Kenneth's face forever? I doubt it, even though our love for each other may stay, eventually we'll separate. The same with Marv, Chris, Brew. Brew's dad said he might move to Pensacola. I dread the thought of losing somebody so close, God. . . .

And next, I'm going to college this year. God, I'm so scared, so afraid . . . I see Mom. God, I don't want to leave her. Sure I want to party, have a place of my own, but I'm so afraid of leaving because I love her and Kari so much.

My Grandparents are going to die soon. I can't see living without . . . God . . . Help. . . .

Football. I'm so scared, I love the game so much. What if I don't make college or a scholarship? It will be the bloody last time to put on a pair of pads, and that hurts . . . BAD.

And Mandy. I love her so much, but, God, I'm not even going to have that forever. . . . I mean, sure, you never know . . . but the only thing that makes me happy and I can talk to might not be here either. And also talking to her about a problem of hers. God, this

Kyle Lynch at his last football game, Nov. 1991.

sucks so bad . . . I love you Mandy. Wherever you may go in the future, I will love all of you . . . Mom, Kari, Marvin, Chris, Kenneth, Alec, Rodrik, Brian,

Travis, Brian, Paul, Bobby, Trey, Brew, Mandy, Luke. . . .

I mean, you know, all I've really, really, really, really got is myself, and then eventually I'm gone.

Well, I'm going. I love everybody. Thanks for listening, piece of paper, or whoever reads it.

Love

Peace

Your Buddy, Lover, Son, Brother   4 ever

I Love U All. . . .

On March 28, Kyle went to a party with some friends. The friend that had driven Kyle to the party had to leave early, so Kyle caught a ride with a young man later that evening when he was ready to go home. The young man, whom Kyle did not know well, had been drinking. Perhaps Kyle didn't realize this when he climbed into the back seat, but it was a mistake that would cost him and his family dearly.

The car carrying Kyle and three other young people was traveling more than 100 miles an hour when the driver lost control in a curve. Police reports estimate that the vehicle slid sideways approximately 130 feet, then went airborne for 46 feet. The 1992 Mustang finally came to a stop with its rear end slamming into a tree. Kyle was thrown from the car through the back window.

Karen answered a knock on the door at 1:00 a.m. and experienced what she now calls "a mother's worst nightmare." She was told that Kyle had been in an accident and was at St. Thomas Hospital in critical condition. When she called the hospital, she was told to come and to bring someone with her. Kari was not home that night, so Karen called a friend and they began what would be the longest trip of her life.

On the way to the hospital, Karen kept thinking of all the hard times she, Kyle, and Kari had shared, and how they had always pulled together to make it through. She just knew in her heart that they would be able to again.

When Karen and her friend arrived at the hospital, she was told she could not see Kyle right away. They anxiously awaited further word on Kyle's condition. Eventually, a doctor came out and told her the words she says she will never be able to forget: "I think you know what I am going to say. We did all we could." Kyle Lynch had died at the age of 18.

Though his pain was over, the pain his mother and his sister would endure had just begun. On Monday, March 30, 1992 (Karen's birthday), a memorial service for Kyle was held in the Hillwood High gymnasium. With all the students, friends, and teachers present, Coach Link presented Karen with Kyle's football jersey, number 82, which they had retired in his honor. He also handed her Kyle's cap and gown, which had just come in for graduation. Karen then spoke to the crowd.

She told Kyle's fellow students—among them many of his closest friends—that they must continue on, and that they must realize how precious life really is. She asked them not to take chances, and to live each day the best way possible.

The last thing Karen did at the memorial service was to play the song *The Dance.* As the music began, Karen looked out into the faces of the young audience. Tears rolled down their cheeks as they remembered Kyle. They reflected upon his bright smile, his crazy sense of humor, his athletic ability — but most of all, the way he seemed to care, really care, about everyone around him. She knew that they all realized, as she did, that it really was worth the pain just to have known him.

As the school year came to a close, Hillwood High School's yearbook was dedicated to Kyle, and his premonition from months before sadly came true. Karen was presented with a yearbook signed by many of his friends and fellow students.

The year following Kyle's death was a hard one for Karen and Kari. Kyle had been more than a son and a brother. He had been "the man of the house" and a best friend to them both, as well as a father figure to Kari. Karen felt a lot of anger toward God for allowing this tragedy to happen.

In a children's story which Karen wrote, entitled *The Storm,* she compared her loss to that of a tree after a raging storm . . .

> *I knew my oldest sapling had been destroyed*
>   *by the storm,*
> *And there I was, leaning, with my life draining.*
> *My roots were so bent and there were no signs*
>   *of life.*
> *I felt barren and alone in my misery.*

Finally, Karen realized that she too must go on for Kari's sake, as well as for the sake of Kyle's memory. She stopped shaking her fist at God and began to reach out to others. She started to share the story of her tragedy, so that others might avoid the same misfortune. She became involved with Mothers Against Drunk Driving (MADD), and began speaking to high school students, as well as to DUI offenders. In her speeches, she tells the story of Kyle's life — and that of his death. It is impossible for her to do so without shedding some tears. Her audience usually joins in. In her speeches, Karen uses the lyrics of *The Dance* to describe her feelings for Kyle: *Holding you I held everything. . . . How was I to know you'd ever say goodbye. . .* and *I could have missed the pain, but I'd of had to miss the dance.*

Each time Karen speaks for MADD, she is forced to relive the pain and suffering she and Kari went through after the accident. She has spoken to over 10,000 young people so far in 1995, and has asked them not to make the wrong decision to drink and drive or to ride in a car with someone who has been drinking. To the DUI offenders, she shares her story in hopes that they will not become repeat offenders. Kari has grown into a beautiful young lady. She graduated from high school and is now attending college. She and Karen have begun a new life with the memories they share of Kyle to strengthen them. Like all his friends, teachers, coaches, and anyone who met this handsome, athletic, full of life, "all-around good guy," they will never forget number 82.

For Kyle Lynch truly did not "miss the dance." And, someday, they will all dance *The Dance* once again.

In 1994, there were 480 fatalities in the state of Tennessee and 17,000 nationwide due to drunk driving accidents. More deadly than any disease or affliction, drunk driving accidents are the #1 killer of young people in our country.

Tennessee Mothers Against Drunk Driving (MADD)
783 Old Harding
Suite 111 East
Brentwood, Tennessee 37027

There's No Way

Alabama

SONGWRITER:
John Jarrard
Lisa Palas
Will Robinson

As I lay by your side and hold you tonight
I want you to understand
This love that I feel is so right and so real
I realize how lucky I am
And should you ever wonder if my love is true
There's something that I want to make clear
   to you

> *Chorus:*
> *There's no way I could make it without you*
> *There's no way that I'd even try*
> *If I had to survive, without you in my life*
> *I knew I wouldn't last a day*
> *Oh, baby, there's no way*

It means so much to me whenever I see
That wanting me look in your eyes
And I don't know how I could do without
Holding you close every night
I've waited so long just to have you to hold
And now that I've got you, I'll never let go

> *Repeat Chorus*

Bridge:
I never knew until you
What I was missing
Now you say forever, and I find
My heart is listenin'
Yes I'm listening

> *Repeat Chorus*

When John Jarrard, Lisa Palas, and Will Robinson were writing the song, *There's No Way*, they thought they were writing a traditional man/woman love song. When the group Alabama recorded the song, they too felt that they were recording a traditional man/woman love song. Their fans had come to expect that type of song from them, and the group had already taken several "love songs" to the #1 position on the charts. *There's No Way* was to be no exception. When lead singer, Randy Owen, wrapped his warm, sensuous voice around the beautiful lyrics of *There's No Way*, he conveyed what every man wants to say to the woman he loves.

To a young man named Tony Moore from Munford, Alabama, the song expressed what he wanted to say to the woman he loved. However, this woman was not his girl friend, his lover, or his wife. Tony did not hear in this song a traditional man/woman love situation. *There's No Way* became his love song to his mother. In Tony's own words, here is the story of what this song meant to him:

My name is Tony Franklin Moore. I was born with spina bifida on October 26, 1972. My parents were asked by the hospital staff if they would put me in a nursing home. They said I wouldn't live anyway, but my parents kept me. The nurse told my parents that if they kept me, I would live longer if I had lots of love. One day I heard this song:

When I lay by your side and hold you tonight,
I want you to understand this love that I feel is so
*   right and so real,*
I realize how lucky I am,
And should you ever wonder if my love is true,
There's something that I want to make clear to
*   you . . .*

There's no way I could make it without you.

You see, I'd lay my head on my mother's chest when I
was little, and she would tell me how much she loved me.
All of my life, she has told me over and over how proud
she was of me and how much she loves me. I sure do feel
her love in the chorus of the song:

There's no way I could make it without you,
There's no way that I'd even try,
If I had to survive, without you in my life,
I know I wouldn't last a day,
Oh, baby [or mom], there's no way.

My dad worked hard so my mother could stay home
and take care of me. I believe that if my parents hadn't
kept me, I would have died. You see, we all need love to
live, and I've had plenty of love in my life—not only from
my parents, but from family, friends, and special people
like Randy Owen of Alabama and my best buddy, John
Jarrard. This is a love song for my mother from me to tell
her how much I love her. There is no way I could make it
without her. The second verse says:

It means so much to me whenever I see,
That wanting me look in your eyes;
And I don't know how I could do without,
Holding you close every night.

I've waited so long just to have you to hold,
And now that I've got you, I'll never let you go . . .

There's no way I could make it without you.

Needless to say, Tony's mom, Hazel Moore, was
moved. The song took on a new meaning for her as
well. In Hazel's own words:

When Tony was born, he was taken from a little country hospital and rushed to a hospital in Birmingham. I
was only allowed to see him through the glass in the
nursery. I didn't get to hold him until he was two
weeks old. I was afraid he wouldn't know that I was
his mother. They would hold him up to the window of
the nursery, so I could see him. His big eyes would
look at me and melt my heart. Tears would drop off
my cheek because I longed to hold my baby. When
we brought him home, I spent lots of time holding
him. Not long after bringing him home, he was back
in the hospital for more surgery. He's had 35 sur-
geries, the first when he was five days old and the last
in February, 1995. Many times I could only hold his
hand, and, looking into his eyes, I would tell him how
much I loved him and needed him to live and
couldn't make it without him. I believe our faith and
strong bond, and the love we have, is why he is alive
today. Can't you see why this song is so special to
us?"

In 1985, when Tony was in the Children's Hospital in Birmingham for yet another surgery, a
woman named Laura Patton came to his room.
Mrs. Patton told Tony about an organization called
Magic Moments, whose purpose is to grant wishes

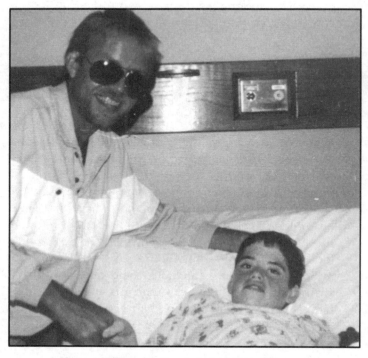

Songwriter John Jarrard and Tony Moore.

to sick and seriously ill children. Tony could ask for anything he wanted or go anywhere he chose. He did not have to think twice. He asked to see Alabama in concert.

Randy Owen of Alabama personally called Tony and informed him that he and the other members of the band would be meeting him soon. Randy also told the youngster that the members of the band were really looking forward to his visit. Magic

Moments planned a weekend trip to Six Flags over Georgia and to Cummings, Georgia, where Alabama would be performing at Lanierland Country Music Park. There Tony was able to meet Randy Owen face to face. They talked for several minutes before Randy went onstage. Randy asked Tony if there was anything he could do for him. Tony requested his favorite song, *There's No Way*, and asked Randy to dedicate it to him and his mom. Owen obliged, and it was a very "Magic Moment" for Tony and his family.

One might expect the story to end there, but it did not. At this juncture, the life-changing aspect of the song *There's No Way* comes into play.

By coincidence, one of the writers of the song, John Jarrard, was in the audience during Tony's Magic Moment. John is no ordinary songwriter. He has had numerous #1's and many other hits before and since writing *There's No Way*. This song became more than just another hit when John met Tony Moore. John Jarrard himself has had many struggles with his health, just as Tony has. John lost his eyesight in 1979 due to complications from diabetes. This came at a time when John was just beginning his songwriting career. When most people in this challenging profession might have given up, even without a disability, John Jarrard continued to hone his songwriting craft. He took a mobility training course and learned to walk with the aid of a cane so that he could get around Music Row and pitch his songs. Soon his dedication, persistence, and perseverance began to pay off. He became a successful songwriter with another Alabama recording, *You've Got the Touch*, becoming his second #1 song. In the 1980s, John established himself as one of the top songwriters in Nashville.

When John met Tony in 1985 at the Alabama concert, a special relationship was born. John encouraged Tony, who had been undergoing many painful medical procedures, not to give up. He told Tony of his blindness and shared how he had worked to overcome the obstacles that were put in his way. Tony's spirits were lifted and he drew from John's strength. John asked Tony's mother Hazel if he could stay in touch with Tony and his family. Of course, Hazel said yes, and the relationship continued by phone throughout the following years. John even flew from Nashville to Birmingham to be by Tony's side for a serious back surgery he had to undergo.

In December of 1990, the tables were turned and John faced another challenge to his health. His kidney and pancreas were failing, and doctors told him he would need a transplant to live. Now it was Tony's turn to be there for John. This time John would draw from Tony's strength.

As he underwent this life-threatening operation, and in the months following when the chance for rejecting his new organs was greatest, John experienced many moments of doubt and depression. At times, he wondered to himself if he would survive; at times he questioned whether or not he wanted to survive. When John reached his lowest emotional state, Tony Moore's inspiration kicked in. John relates, "Whenever I felt robbed, I would think of Tony, and I knew that no matter what I was going through, Tony had been through worse."

John did survive and is still writing hits today.

In 1994 alone, he had four top-ten records (*What's in It for Me?* by John Berry; *Sure Can Smell the Rain* by Blackhawk; *We Can't Love Like This*, another hit for Alabama; and *My Kind of Girl* by Collin Raye).

Tony Moore continues to survive as well. His condition is presently stable. His mother Hazel and the rest of his family and friends are still there to provide constant support, and, most importantly — love. Tony remains a big country music fan. And though he has enjoyed many songs over the years, *There's No Way* remains his favorite.

For John Jarrard and Tony Moore, the song *There's No Way* will forever be a bond between them.

Magic Moments
c/o Children's Hospital of Alabama
1600 7th Avenue South
Birmingham, Alabama 35233

Achy-Breaky Heart

Billy Ray Cyrus

SONGWRITER:
Don Von Tress

You can tell the world you never was my girl
You can burn my clothes up when I'm gone
You can tell your friends just what a fool I've been
And laugh and joke about me on the phone
You can tell my arms go back to the farm
You can tell my feet to hit the floor
Or you can tell my lips to tell my fingertips
They won't be reaching out for you no more

Chorus:
But don't tell my heart
My achy-breaky heart
I just don't think he'd understand
And if you tell my heart
My achy-breaky heart
He might blow up and kill this man

You can tell my Ma I moved to Arkansas
You can tell your dog to bite my leg
Or tell your brother Cliff whose fist can tell my lip
He never really liked me anyway
Or tell your Aunt Louise, tell anything you please
Myself already knows I'm not okay
Or you can tell my eyes to watch out for my mind
I might be walking out on him today

Repeat Chorus

Instrumental

Repeat Chorus x 2

Much of the research for this book came in the form of letters from many country music artists' fan club members. No club responded with more enthusiasm than the members of Billy Ray Cyrus' fan club. After the article soliciting stories for *Songs That Changed Our Lives* appeared in Billy Ray's fan club newsletter, *The Spirit*, we received hundreds of letters from his fans across the United States and around the world.

They sent stories about Billy Ray's tribute song to American veterans, *Some Gave All*. They sent stories about his touching ballad, *She's Not Crying Anymore*. They wrote about the passionate *It Could've Been Me*, and the poignant *Storm in the Heartland*.

But the song we received more letters about than any other Billy Ray Cyrus hit was the one that made him a worldwide phenomenon — his debut smash, *Achy-Breaky Heart*.

Don Von Tress wrote *Achy-Breaky Heart* in early 1990. At that time, Don was hanging wallpaper for a living. He began composing the song while driving around in his van from one job site to another. As Don tells it . . .

"I spent about 80% of my time on the road driving between jobs. Most of that time was spent writing. I remember singing the chorus of *Achy-Breaky Heart* into a little tape recorder and thinking I had something pretty good. When I got home that night, I pulled out my new guitar and the amplifier I had gotten for Christmas of 1989. The new guitar had really inspired my writing [something Don had been pursuing since 1963 with little success], and the signature guitar riff of the song came pretty quickly. When I finished the song that night — some people may think this is crazy — but I distinctly remember having a clear vision of little kids singing and dancing. It was overwhelming, and I felt then that *Achy-Breaky Heart* was going to be special."

The simple, almost nursery-rhyme lyric about a fellow who gives his soon-to-be ex-lover a list of options she can take once he is gone, had a humorous charm.

The two-chord melody and infectious rhythm were undeniably catchy. Anyone from age three to 93 could sing along effortlessly. It was an easy song to like . . . and dislike.

Achy-Breaky Heart was ravaged by the critics. Travis Tritt said aloud what many other country artists were whispering under their breath — that this song did not represent country music, nor did Billy Ray Cyrus have any right to call himself a country artist.

But Billy Ray's fans didn't care what the critics, or Tritt, said. They turned out in droves at his concerts and at the record stores. The *Some Gave All* album soared past platinum sales of 1,000,000 and continues selling today with a total sales figure of close to 10,000,000.

In the letters we received from Billy Ray Cyrus' fans, they spoke of how *Achy-Breaky Heart* had miraculously helped cure physical ailments and end lonely bouts of depression. It had even served as the impetus for one woman's 100-pound weight loss. Many people wrote that they had never been country music fans until they heard Billy Ray, and were converted by his rock-tinged, "twang-less" vocals. Scores of young people, from toddlers to teenagers, those traditionally not a prime listening audience for country music, became infected by the "Cyrus Virus."

One of these new young fans was 11-year-old Brooke Gall of Susquehanna, Pennsylvania.

Brooke covered her bedroom with Billy Ray posters. There she spent hour after hour listening to his music. She wore Billy Ray T-shirts and watched CMT (Country Music Television), eagerly awaiting each time they would air a Billy Ray video.

Brooke Gall was like millions of other preteen girls—a Billy Ray fanatic. But unlike most of the other young girls, Brooke is different. She is indeed a special fan—for Brooke is a Down Syndrome child.

One of the more serious characteristics of Down Syndrome can be heart defects. Brooke had her first heart surgery at 16 months of age when doctors were forced to repair holes between the chambers of her heart.

Her second heart surgery took place on September 24, 1992, just three months after her eleventh birthday. Brooke had contracted a virus which attacks the heart. The virus caused scar tissue to form on the walls of her heart valve. Surgery was scheduled to repair at least the valve, or possibly to replace it. Prior to the surgery, doctors decided that the valve had to be replaced. The procedure was going to be very risky, with Brooke facing only a 50-50 chance of survival.

Billy Ray Cyrus and Brooke Gall.

Brooke traveled to University Hospital in Syracuse, New York, which was 90 miles from her home in Susquehanna. Her mother and stepfather, Mr. and Mrs. Scott Cooper, checked into the Ronald McDonald House near the hospital in order to be by Brooke's side for support. Her grandparents, Mr. and Mrs. Elton Tyler, stayed nearby so that they could be there for Brooke as well.

The day Brooke was admitted to the hospital, she wore her favorite outfit. It wasn't a lacy dress, or a fancy skirt and blouse, but rather her prized possession — A Billy Ray Cyrus Achy-Breaky T-shirt.

Her family waited anxiously as the surgery began. Hours later, the operation was successfully completed. Brooke was then placed on a respirator and given morphine and a paralyzer. Her family began perhaps the most difficult wait, to see if Brooke's young body could survive the stress of the operation.

Brooke was unresponsive the first day after the surgery. The second day came and went uneventfully. Brooke remained on the respirator and was unresponsive. On the third day there were still no signs of consciousness. Late on the fourth day following the surgery, the doctors were becoming increasingly concerned with Brooke's failure to respond. They discussed performing a tracheotomy, another surgical procedure that would tax Brooke's already susceptible body. The doctors finally asked the family if there was something, anything, they could think of which Brooke might possibly respond to. Brooke's family had exactly what the doctor ordered. The *Some Gave All* cassette by Billy Ray Cyrus.

On the fifth day, as Brooke was on the downside of her dose of paralyzer, her family watched as they started the cassette on *Achy-Breaky Heart*. After being totally immobile for five days, Brooke — only seconds after hearing the song — began to sway her arms in a dancing motion while still in her hospital bed, on the respirator. Within an hour, Brooke was off the respirator, sitting up in the bed and asking for some McDonald's french fries.

At 4:00 a.m. the following morning, Brooke remained wide awake and had all the nurses in the cardiac care unit enthusiastically "boogyin'" with her to Billy Ray's music.

A short time later, Brooke had recuperated sufficiently from her surgery to allow her to leave the hospital. As she walked out of the hospital, she wore yet another special T-shirt, one which her family had custom-made for her during her hospital stay. The words they had imprinted on the shirt said what Brooke's smile reflected: "MY ACHY-BREAKY HEART IS ALL BETTER NOW."

Once Brooke had fully recuperated from her operation, she had one thing on her mind: meeting Billy Ray Cyrus in person. Brooke's grandmother wrote to Billy Ray's manager, Jack McFadden, and told him the story of Brooke's miraculous recovery. Billy Ray was to be in Binghamton, New York, on November 3, 1993, for a concert. Arrangements were made for Brooke and her family to attend the show and meet Billy Ray backstage.

Their tickets were three rows from the stage, but evidently Billy Ray knew where his biggest fan was sitting that night. Brooke's mom, Larena, says Billy Ray spent 90% of the concert right in front of Brooke. He even tossed one of his coveted towels, used to wipe his brow, directly to Brooke.

Afterward, the entire family went backstage. Brooke was beside herself at the prospect of meeting her idol, but she was not shy. She asked to sing *Achy-Breaky Heart* together with Billy Ray. There has never been a more touching duet. Brooke then presented Billy Ray with a rose she had brought to the concert. Billy Ray was genuinely moved. He proved it by asking, "Brooke, do you like flowers?" When Brooke replied, "Yes," Billy Ray scooped up every rose he had been given that night by hundreds of fans and gave them all to Brooke.

As Brooke left the arena that night, she was smiling just as she had been when she left the hospital a year earlier. She was once again wearing a T-shirt. A picture of Billy Ray Cyrus was on the front, and on the back was the title of her favorite song, *Achy-Breaky Heart*. A simple, childlike song—yet it has touched millions, and has perhaps saved the life of one: Brooke Gall.

Central New York—Ronald McDonald House
1027 E. Genesee Street
Syracuse, New York 13210

How Can I Help You To Say Goodbye

Patty Loveless

SONGWRITER:
Burton B. Collins
Karen Taylor-Good

Through the back window of our '59 wagon
I watched my best friend Jamie slippin' further away
I kept on wavin' till I couldn't see her
Through my tears I asked again why we couldn't stay
Mama whispered softly, "Time will ease your pain . . .
Life's about changing. Nothing ever stays the same."
  And she said

> *Chorus:*
> *How can I help you to say goodbye*
> *It's OK to hurt, and it's OK to cry*
> *Come let me hold you, and I will try*
> *How can I help you . . . to say goodbye*

I sat on our bed, he packed his suitcase
I held a picture of our wedding day
His hands were trembling, we both were crying
He kissed me gently, and then he quickly walked away
I called up Mama, she said "Time will ease your pain . . .
Life's about changing, nothing ever stays the same."
  And she said

  Repeat Chorus

Sittin' with Mama, alone in her bedroom
She opened her eyes, and then squeezed my hand
She said "I have to go now, my time here is over"
And with her final words she tried to help me understand
Mama whispered softly, "Time will ease your pain . . .
Life's about changing, nothing ever stays the same."
  And she said

  Repeat Chorus

The inspiration for the beautiful song, *How Can I Help You Say Goodbye*, came from a real-life incident in the life of one of the song's writers, Burton Collins. Burton shared the story of this experience in a letter he wrote to Patty Loveless, the artist whose tender rendition of the song became one of her biggest hits.

Dear Patty,

My grandmother, Sarah, was my best friend. We laughed together, danced together, sang and cried together. We shared the secrets of our souls. I miss her.

In January of 1988, she was diagnosed with inoperable cancer and emphysema. Her doctor, who had been her friend for over 30 years, told her that he could keep her alive on drugs and treatments for approximately 6 months to a year, or he could give her a transfusion, which would make her feel great for two days, and she'd be dead in four. She opted for the latter. Sarah called my dad and asked him to invite the family down to her house for a last reunion.

For two days, we all sat around her bed laughing and telling stories. She had the most beautiful blue eyes, and they still sparkled when she laughed. Though she was hooked up to a respirator and flat on her back, she never lost her dignity or zest for life and family.

At the end of the second day she told us it was time to go. One by one we all said goodbye.

When it was my turn, I sat beside her on the bed and gently held her hand. I was trying as hard as I could to hold back my tears. She gave my hand a little pat and said, "It's OK." She told me she was a little scared, and I said I was too. I knew when I walked out of that bedroom, it would be for the very last time. Rarely in life do you know when the last time is, and I knew. She had a way of understanding what I was going through, and she smiled at me and whispered, "How can I help you say goodbye?" I said, "Just hold me." She reached up to me and said, "Come here, sweetie," and for the last time she held me in those lovin' arms that held me all my life. I told her I loved her, kissed her gently on the forehead, then walked out the door.

She died two days later with my mother at her side, listening to the song, *Try to Remember.*

How Can I Help You Say Goodbye is my tribute to my best friend who will always be with me.

As Sarah always said, "Sing pretty, and don't fall off the stage."

May God Bless You,
Burton Collins

In an open letter that Patty Loveless wrote, which was used in the record company promotion for *How Can I Help You Say Goodbye* she tells the story behind her decision to record the song. . .

Dear Music Lover,

When Emory, my husband and producer, first brought me *How Can I Help You Say Goodbye,* I knew it was a song I had to sing. Moving through three of life's toughest challenges, it touched me because it quietly cut to the heart of getting through it all; having the often unseen and unacknowledged support of unconditional love.

As a child, I've moved away from friends and know that ache. I've been through all the emotions of knowing a marriage isn't going to make it and had to accept that defeat. I've lost my father, a man who was always a tremendous source of strength and inspiration for me. Letting go isn't an easy thing to do.

We have all experienced these things. Somehow we survive. That's why I had to sing *How Can I Help You Say Goodbye*. It offers us strength and hope.

I had no idea how difficult it was going to be for me to perform it in the studio. I had just recovered from emergency vocal surgery that could have meant the end of my career. I was so emotionally overwhelmed that I kept breaking down while I was singing.

In an attempt to get me through this process, Burton Banks Collins, the song's writer, wrote me a letter about how the song came to be written. For him, it was about how his grandmother helped him face those turning points in life.

And that's the thing about this song. Everyone has been here and felt these emotions. There's no lonelier, more isolated feeling, you're sure at that moment, nothing will ever hurt more.

Those are the times you need to know you're not alone. There are pillars of strength around you no matter what you're going through, you just have to look, or listen.

As a young woman, many times I found strength and hope in the music I loved and listened to. Maybe this song can do that for others—that's my hope.

Patty

In Monticello, Arkansas, Karen and Jason Caldwell needed all the strength and hope they could find.

Their daughter, Taylor Melinda Caldwell, was born on February 8, 1993. The joy and excitement of having their first child soon turned to fear and heartbreak. Within 12 hours, Taylor was moved from the local hospital in Monticello to a larger medical facility with specialized care capabilities in Little Rock, Arkansas.

Taylor was a beautiful, happy baby, but there was one problem. She was afflicted with a disorder that caused her body to be much like that of a Raggedy Ann doll. She was unable to push herself up or raise her head. Her arms and legs simply "flopped" when she was picked up, and she had to be totally supported by the person holding her.

Jason and Karen were able to bring Taylor home from the hospital when she was nine days old, but were forced to make constant trips back for numerous tests as the doctors tried to diagnose her condition. After nine long and frustrating months, the Caldwells received the diagnosis. Taylor had a muscle disorder called Congenital Fibertype Disproportion. According to the specialists at the hospital, the next few months would be crucial to Taylor's survival. The Caldwells were told that if she could make it through the bad respiratory months (flu and pneumonia months), Taylor might be slow, but her lifespan would be normal.

Jason and Karen had hope as Taylor approached her first birthday in February of 1994. Unfortunately, Taylor ended up spending most of that month in the Arkansas Children's Hospital with a severe case of a respiratory bacteria called RSV. She was on a respirator for 10 days, and when she finally got to come home, Jason and Karen had to attach their daughter to a breathing machine at night.

In June, Taylor again contracted pneumonia and was in the hospital for five days. After this episode, Karen took Taylor out of daycare and started taking her to work with her each day in hopes it would decrease her chances of infection.

Taylor seemed to improve for a short time, as Karen worked two days a week and accompanied Taylor to physical and occupational therapy three times each week. She was sitting up for three to five minutes at a time and actually progressing in her development. Karen and Jason finally had a reason to believe the specialists' prognosis that Taylor would have a normal lifespan and, perhaps, a somewhat normal life.

But it was not to be. Taylor's condition took a turn for the worse as she was again stricken with pneumonia. On September 7, 1994, Karen could tell that her baby was in trouble. Her body was weak and tired from the struggle she had endured. Karen called Jason to come home from work so they could take Taylor to the children's hospital once again. Deep inside they both realized it would probably be her last day.

As Karen and Taylor waited for Jason to arrive, they had a "talk." Karen softly told her young daughter that she had been put through enough and was a brave little girl. It was time for her to do what she wanted to do. If she could no longer fight this battle, her mommy and daddy would miss her terribly . . . but they would always love her.

As Jason and Karen sat holding Taylor in the emergency room, she looked up at them. All of their friends had always said that Taylor's eyes said everything. Even when she was in pain, Taylor rarely cried. But this time, her eyes filled with tears, and as a couple of them streamed down her face, Karen caught them on her fingertips. She gave one to Jason and whispered to Taylor that they "would keep them forever." The last words they said to their child were, "We'll love you and we'll miss you." Taylor passed away in her mother's arms with her father by her side.

The Caldwells had decided to donate Taylor's organs and were able to give someone her corneas and heart valves. As Karen says today, "This way somebody else has a chance to live and keep a part of Taylor alive."

Karen had first seen the video of *How Can I Help You Say Goodbye* on CMT (Country Music Television) several weeks before Taylor passed away. As she continued to hear the song up until Taylor's death, it was a comfort and an aid in helping her, as well as Jason, accept Taylor's "letting go."

They decided to have the song sung at Taylor's funeral. The first and last verses were used because, as Karen says, "The first verse was appropriate because pretty much everyone has moved away and lost touch with a close friend. To some, Taylor was a friend who always had a smile. The last verse was fitting because everyone will sooner or later have to say good-bye to a loved one. Taylor was everybody's little girl. In my eyes, this was my

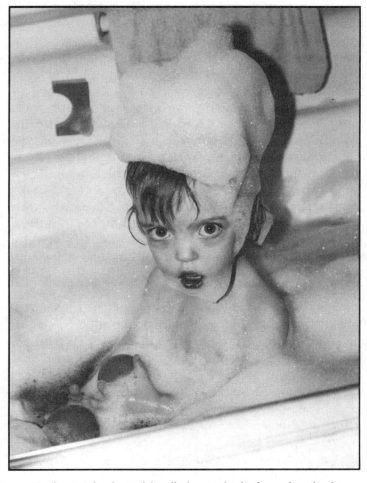

Taylor Melinda Caldwell the night before she died.

song to everyone. My comfort to our friends and Taylor's extended family."

Melissa Barnes McBee was chosen to sing *How Can I Help You Say Goodbye*. She had sung *I Will Always Love You* at Karen and Jason's wedding. Neither she, nor the rest of the people at the church, were able to make it through the song without tears.

In November of 1994, Karen and Jason were able to meet Burton Collins' mother in Monticello, coincidentally the hometown of Mrs. Collins. The Caldwells told her how much Burton's song meant to them and continued to help in their healing process. Mrs. Collins later shared the letter Burton had written to Patty Loveless with Karen and Jason. It was apparent to them that the feelings Burton had experienced when he had to face his grandmother's death were similar to the feelings they had about losing their nineteen-month-old infant.

As Burton had poured his heart into the writing of *How Can I Help You Say Goodbye* in tribute to his grandmother Sarah Banks Polk, Karen expressed her emotions regarding Taylor's death with a prose poem entitled *I Can't Look, I Can See*. The following are excerpts from that poem.

I can't look at my husband without seeing great pain in the loss of our daughter. . . . I can see in my husband the wonderful, loving daddy he was and how he did everything for his little girl.

I can't look at her pictures without feeling lost and hurt. . . . I can see in her pictures the love and hope I had for her and her future.

I can't look at my arms without seeing my baby

leaving us and going into Heaven. . . . I can see in my arms my daughter and how she depended on them for support and strength from the day she entered into this world.

I can't look at other babies without remembering my joy of seeing my little girl and my hurt that I couldn't hold her 24 hours a day if I wanted to. . . . I can see in other babies and know the joy and pride their parents have for bringing something so precious into this world.

I can't look at other children, for in them I visualize what my daughter might be doing today. . . . I can see from other children the hope I have in the future. For one of them may be the scientist who discovers the cure for my daughter's disorder.

I can't look at my friends without seeing hurt and compassion. For my daughter was theirs too. They shared our joys, accomplishments and disappointments, no matter what, they were there. . . . I can see in my friends how one little girl may have changed their lives, whether it may have been enjoying a loved one more or being patient with a disabled person, or just learning how to smile.

I can't look at the sunset, for when a sun sets it is the end of a day and everybody has one day when the sun will set and we will die. . . . I can see beyond a sunset, for when a sunset happens there is a sunrise on a new day. Now my daughter is where the sunsets and sunrises are beyond expression. One day I will be able to see them with her.

As one of Karen's closest friends, Robin Mc-
Clendon, said of Taylor's passing, "Everyone is put
on this earth for a purpose. Sometimes people are
born knowing what that purpose is. It seems Taylor was one of those who knew exactly why she was
here. Her personality was pure charm and her
smile brought delight to even the grumpiest of people. The smallest accomplishment for healthy
babies was a grand feat for Taylor, Karen, and Jason. And once a hurdle was overcome it was often
hard to tell who was most proud — Taylor or mom
or dad.

"Taylor's brief stay here taught many of us lessons. To many, that a smile, no matter how tough
life got, was a way to get beyond the day. To others, Taylor's condition reminded us of the fragility
and brevity of life — therefore reminding us to make
the most of each moment. But I think the most important lesson Taylor's life taught was to her parents, Jason and Karen, who learned how to be
strong, how to love and lose, and how to keep from
becoming bitter in an often cold and cruel world.

"Taylor seemed to know that she was here to
teach us all. She was intelligent, happy and calm.
She had a serenity about her that made her seem
very wise and almost angelic. She had no time for
tears, only life lessons. . . and she taught us well."

Karen and Jason continue their healing today,
as they observed the first anniversary of Taylor's
death on September 7. Each time they hear the
song, *How Can I Help You Say Goodbye*, the hope
and strength they gained from it during the 19
months Taylor lived helps them to deal with her
dying. In Karen's words: "Even though each day is

a new day, the memories are still there. When I hear the song, it helps me to realize that, while I am hurting, there are other people hurting. But in time our pain will ease and life will go on. We are just fortunate to have had Taylor for the short time that we did."

Muscular Dystrophy Association
1400 West Markham
Suite 351
Little Rock, Arkansas 72201
Mark envelope:
"For Research—In Memory of Taylor Caldwell"

Love Can Build A Bridge

The Judds

Songwriter:
Naomi Judd
John Jarvis
Paul Overstreet

I'd gladly walk across the desert
With no shoes upon my feet
To share with you the last bite
Of bread I had to eat.
I would swim out to save you
In your sea of broken dreams
When all your hopes are sinking
Let me show you what love means.

> *Chorus:*
> *Love can build a bridge*
> *Between your heart and mine*
> *Love can build a bridge*
> *Don't you think it's time?*
> *Don't you think it's time?*

I would whisper love so loudly
Every heart could understand
That love and only love
Can join the tribes of man
I would give my hearts desire
So that you could see
The first step is to realize
That it all begins with you and me.

Repeat Chorus

Bridge:
When we stand together
It's our finest hour
We can do anything, anything, anything
If we keep believin' in the power.

The song *Love Can Build a Bridge* was one of the biggest hits ever in the career of a duo which became one of most successful acts in country music history. The mother and daughter team known as "The Judds" paired the soft, haunting harmony of the mother, Naomi Judd, with the raw, soulful lead vocal of her daughter, Wynonna.

Naomi also contributed to the success of the Judds with her songwriting ability, penning many of their hits, including *Love Can Build a Bridge*. In her autobiography of the same title, Naomi relates how the song was inspired one day while she was taking a walk in a small town in Oregon:

> I stopped to rest on a park bench across from a homeless man stretched out asleep. Staring at him for the longest time, I wondered such things as what happened to him when he needs medical attention or if anyone knows or cares how or even where he is! If sanity is containing or controlling our confusion, perhaps this fella just didn't keep the lid on his confusion well enough to suit those around him. I remembered how perilously close to being on the streets the kids and I had often been. My unanswered questions and the image of that man sleeping out in the open on a park bench in dirty rags haunted me for days.
>
> My sense of helplessness in the face of suffering is at times so overwhelming I have to vent it in some fashion. I had long noticed that when I write, I create an alternative world and give reality to experience. Wynonna and I had witnessed so much of man's inhu-

manity to man in our odyssey across the United States, but how does one express such things in mere words within the confines of a three-minute song? I can no more make myself write than I can lift my refrigerator. I just waited.

Lying in the dark, being jostled in my bed on the bus the next night, the words showed up, in sudden illuminations like the flickering lights of passing trucks.

I'd gladly walk across the desert with no shoes upon my feet, to share with you the last bite of bread I had to eat. I would even swim out to save you in your sea of broken dreams; when all your hopes are sinking, let me show you what love means. I was happy with this first verse 'cause I believe dreams and hopes are as important to our survival as food, water, clothing, and air.

Country/Christian singer/songwriter Paul Overstreet was having supper with Larry and me one night at our home. We were just discussing how imagination springs forth from the fertile womb of the human spirit, when Paul spied a postcard of the Grand Canyon from Ashley on our refrigerator door. Looking at it closely he made the observation that "sometimes the only way we can cross life's great divides is to let love be a bridge." I knew this was the missing piece in my puzzle.

I phoned Paul the next morning to thank him for the idea, and let him know I was giving him equal credit as a co-writer. "I can't accept that," he argued loudly. "Ideas run the world!" I insisted. "They make the difference between war and peace."

The following day I was cooling off at a sidewalk cafe in Rhode Island. I listened to two guys sitting next to me arguing. The older man's facts were right, but his tone was so brusque his son was obviously shutting him out. I smiled to myself, reflecting on how I'd finally come to the realization that the only way I ever got through to Wy and Ashley is when I stayed calm, rational, and loving. Walking back to our motel, the second verse and chorus came to me.

I would whisper love so loudly every heart could understand, that love and only love can join the tribes of man. I would give my heart's desire if only you could see, the first step is to realize that it all begins with you and me. Love can build a bridge between your heart and mine. Love can build a bridge, don't you think it's time? With *the first step is to realize, it all begins with you and me,* I was suggesting in essence, "It's better to light one small candle than to curse the darkness."

The *Love Can Build a Bridge* album would be the last studio album for the Judds, as Naomi Judd announced her retirement from the group in October of 1990 due to a life-threatening liver disease.

On December 4, 1991, the Judds staged their final concert on live pay-per-view television.

Judy Shepherd of Henrietta, New York, was not a big country music fan at the time, but because her husband, Bob, was, she decided to order the Judds' pay-per-view concert as a present to him for their 29th wedding anniversary.

It proved to be an occasion which would have a dramatic effect on Judy's life. As she watched the concert that night, she now describes how it touched her:

As the concert started, I was interested only in

how Naomi and Wynonna would handle the emotions of appearing together professionally for the last time. As the concert progressed, I honed in on the obvious love the two felt for each other and how they tried to support each other. When they finished singing *Love Can Build a Bridge* (encore), I felt that something momentous had happened to me, but I was not sure what that was. I knew I was glad we had taped the concert and, in the next weeks, replayed the concert ten times.

A little explanation on my background is necessary here. I was adopted as a child and had spent my adulthood wanting, but not courageous enough, to search for my birth family. An adoptee wants to search for many reasons, some of which are medical information, ethnic background, seeing someone who looks like you—answering the "Why?" and "Who am I?" questions.

The concert showed me, I believe, what mother/daughter love can be. Without the *Love Can Build a Bridge* encore, however, I would have yearned a little for such a relationship (my adoptive mother and I were opposites, and although we loved each other, we were never very close)—and that would have been it. However, *Love Can Build a Bridge* spoke directly to my heart with the message that, although I was now 51 and my birth mother, if still alive, was probably in her seventies, it would not matter: 1) the length of time we had been separated, 2) the reason(s) for my adoption, and 3) if she initially rejected contact. The natural love between a parent and child, and between siblings (if there were any) would help resolve problems caused by a reunion. The song's message, and my husband's encouragement, gave me the strength to begin a search for my birth mother.

Judy Shepherd was born in 1940 to an unwed mother, Hazel Mott. Hazel was barely 19 years old; and with just a third grade education, she could only find work as an unskilled laborer, mainly doing cleaning jobs. In addition, the stigma of being an unwed mother was great in those days, and brought disgrace to the family. Hazel decided to put the daughter she had named Rose Mae in a foster home. She had hopes of establishing a home of her own so that she could, in time, reclaim her child. After three years had passed, Hazel was convinced that it would be in Rose Mae's best interest to remain with her foster family. Reluctantly, she put her daughter up for adoption.

Sydney and Eugenia Jaynes adopted Rose Mae at the age of three and a half and changed her name to Judith Ann, calling her "Judy." Judy was raised in the city of Elmira, New York, until she was eight, when her family moved to a dairy farm outside of Horseheads, New York. Though she had two siblings, her parents' biological children, her brother Robert was 13 years older, and her sister Evelyn Jean was eight years older. Both of Judy's adoptive parents had no brothers or sisters, so her extended family was limited to a few great aunts and uncles, with no cousins. Sydney and Eugenia were both hard workers, and they instilled in Judith Ann the values of work and honesty, plus a love for nature and animals. They also provided her with a loving, secure, and happy childhood.

Still Judy felt something was missing. When

she was six years old, a classmate on the playground teased her about being adopted. Judy went home hysterical and confused, seeking answers from her parents. The Jayneses offered comfort but no information.

Judy finally got confirmation of her adoption when her parents gave her the adoption papers after she graduated from college in 1962. While Judy had been in college, she became engaged to Bob Shepherd, a boy she had first met back in the third grade. They married soon after her graduation as Bob completed his first four years of Navy duty. Bob's being a career Navy man required Bob and Judy to constantly be on the move. They were transferred 19 times during their first seventeen years of marriage.

When Bob retired from the Navy in 1980, after 22 years, the couple settled down in New York again with their two adopted sons, Craig and Rodney. They continued to be active, with Bob finishing his Bachelor of Science degree in Hospital Administration and taking a position at St. Mary's Hospital. Judy began her own home-based word processing business in 1984.

Their life was full, but Judy still felt a void. Her adoptive father died in 1986, and her adoptive mother passed away in 1987. Her brother, Robert, had died of a heart attack in 1982. The only member of her immediate family left was her sister, Evelyn Jean. Craig and Rodney had grown up and were leaving home.

The Judds' final concert sparked a new beginning for Judy Shepherd. As she watched Naomi and Wynonna close their show with *Love Can Build a Bridge*, she thought how she would love to have that type of relationship with her birth mother. It was at that point that she began her search for the woman she had not seen in 51 years.

The adoption papers Judy had received after graduating from college contained her mother's maiden name, Hazel Mott, and Judy's birth name, Rose Mae Mott. Her adoptive parents had told her that her mother was from Cortland, New York. Using telephone book listings, she began to write letters to all the Motts she could find listed. She had several false alarms; but within five weeks, she finally got the name and address of a Hazel Mott Slate in Binghamton, New York, who was the right age.

She called information for Hazel's phone number and then nervously dialed it. Judy now recalls praying, "Dear God, let this be the right decision."

When Hazel answered the phone, Judy apprehensively explained why she was calling. After asking a few questions regarding Hazel's maiden name and whether or not she had ever lived in Newark, New York, Judy asked the question that she had prayed for so long to have answered: "Did she have a daughter born on April 9, 1940, named Rose Mae that she put up for adoption?" When Hazel said "Yes," Judy knew she had finally found her "Mom."

Hazel and Judy talked for almost half an hour, and a lot of Judy's questions began to get answers. She found out that she was the eldest of nine children, with seven of them still living. Her sister Patricia had been killed in an automobile accident

Judy Shepherd and her birth family. back row: Donald, Joyce and Raymond. front row: Elizabeth, Irine, Judy, Kathryn (Kitty). front: Hazel

several years earlier; and her youngest brother, Thomas, had died shortly after birth. She also learned that her four sisters and two brothers had given her an extended family of five sisters and brothers-in-law, 21 nieces and nephews, and three great-nieces and nephews.

After Judy had spoken with her mom, she called Kitty, one of the sisters she had just discovered she had. Kitty said to Judy, "What took you so long to find us? I love you." This was a theme that was to be repeated every time Judy established contact with another member of her birth family. Judy then called her husband Bob to share the news with him, and together they cried on the phone. Less than two weeks later, on March 14, 1992, Judy and Bob traveled to Binghamton to meet her family. Judy first wanted to spend some time alone with her mother. They talked for almost an hour as they looked through family photo albums. Judy was thrilled to learn that her grandfather was an Iroquois Indian.

Next, they drove to her sister Kitty's house nearby, and Judy met three of her sisters and their families. When they compared school pictures, a strong family resemblance was evident. It was an emotional reunion.

Later in March, Judy's eldest brother, Raymond, came from Rhode Island to meet her. Then, in April, she and Bob went to Erie, Pennsylvania, to meet her eldest sister, Joyce, and her family.

On April 9, Judy got her first opportunity to share her birthday with the woman who had brought her into the world. She sent Hazel (by that time she was calling her "Mom") flowers, thanking her for "the precious gift of life." She gave her roses in honor of her birth name, Rose Mae.

In May of 1992, Judy spent her first Mother's Day with her mother, joining the entire family at a reunion at her sister Irine's house. There Judy finally met her other brother, Don, and his family. It was the first time her birth family had been together in over 17 years. . . and this time they had a new member—their sister Judy.

Because her birth family had not been able to attend Judy's wedding, she and Bob decided to renew their vows on their 30th anniversary in 1992. They had rarely attended church in over 17 years, but felt that they should, before reenacting the ceremony. As a result of their visits, Judy and Bob once again became active in church activities and now attend services regularly. *Love Can Build a Bridge* was very much a part of their celebration in renewing their vows. It was played before the service and as theme music for the party afterward.

Judy had sent Naomi Judd a flower arrangement with a thank-you note on the day she found her birth mother. On the day she met her mother and three sisters, they all wrote thank-you messages on a card and mailed it to Naomi.

Judy found a copy of the sheet music for *Love Can Build a Bridge* and got it autographed by Naomi, her co-writers Paul Overstreet and John Jarvis, and Wynonna. It is now framed in her living room with a picture of her birth mother and the rest of the family taken at their first reunion.

Judy now says that bonding with her birth family has not always been easy:

"The first six months or so I was constantly

playing the song (*Love Can Build A Bridge*), plus the Judds' *Guardian Angels* and *River of Time*. Thanks to the message of the song (with love you can overcome obstacles) and the adoption support group we found after the reunion, I was able to pull out of the severe depression I had experienced due to the circumstances of my birth, Mom not looking for me, etc. She had been 'brainwashed,' as are most birth mothers, to think she had no right to search for me, even after I was an adult. Therefore, even though she had my adoptive family's name and city of residence, she never did try to contact me. It took me a long time to 'forgive' her for not trying all those years."

But as Judy Shepherd has learned, *Love Can Build a Bridge*. Her love gave her the strength to cross a bridge that led her to find the family she might never have known she had.

International Soundex Reunion Registry
P.O. Box 2312
Carson City, Nevada 89702-2312
(National clearing agency where adoptees and
birth families can register for possible reunion)

The Mississippi Squirrel Revival

Ray Stevens

SONGWRITER:
C.W. Kalb, Jr.
Carlene Kalb

When I was a kid I'd take a trip every summer
down to Mississippi
To visit my Granny in her antebellum world
I'd run barefooted all day long climbin' trees free
as a song
And one day I happened to catch myself a
squirrel
I stuffed him down in an old shoe box,
punched a couple of holes in the top
And when Sunday came I snuck him into church
I was sittin' way back on the very last pew show-
in' him to my good buddy Hugh
When that squirrel got loose and went totally
berserk
What happened next is hard to tell
Some thought it was heaven others thought it
was hell
But the fact that something was among us was
plain to see
As the choir sang "I Surrender All" the squirrel
ran up Harv Newlan's coveralls
Harv leaped to his feet and said "Something's
got a hold of me" Hallelujah!

Chorus:
The day the squirrel went berserk in the First
Self Righteous Church
In the sleepy little town of Pascagoula

It was a fight for survival that broke out in revival
They was jumpin' pews and shoutin' Hallelujah!

Harv hit the aisles dancin' and screamin'
Some thought he had religion others thought he had a
    demon
And Harv thought he had a weed eater loose in his Fruit-of-
    the-Looms
He fell to his knees to plead and beg and the squirrel ran out
    of his britches leg
Unobserved to the other side of the room
All the way to the amen pew where sat Sister Bertha-Better-
    Than-You
Who'd been watchin all the commotion with sadistic glee
But you should've seen the look in her eyes
When the squirrel jumped her garters and crossed her thighs
She jumped to her feet and said "Lord have mercy on me"
As the squirrel made laps inside her dress
She began to cry and then to confess to sins that would make
    a sailor blush with shame
She told of gossip and church dissension but the thing that
    got the most attention
Was when she talked about her love life and started naming
    names

   Repeat Chorus

Well seven deacons and the pastor got saved,
Twenty-five thousand dollars was raised and fifty volunteered
For missions in the Congo on the spot
Even without an invitiation there were at least five hundred
    rededications
And we all got baptized whether we needed it or not
Now you've heard the Bible story I guess
How He parted the waters for Moses to pass
Oh the miracles God has wrought in this old world
But the one I'll remember 'til my dyin' day
Is how He put that church back on the narrow way
With a half crazed Mississippi squirrel

   Repeat Chorus

Whose life did Ray Stevens' recording of *Mississippi Squirrel Revival* change, you ask?

We thought it would be interesting to include one chapter in this book about the person or persons whose lives are most altered every time a song becomes a hit — the writer or writers of the hit song . . . especially when it's the writer's first big hit. This was the case for the writers of *Mississippi Squirrel Revival*, husband and wife Buddy and Carlene Kalb. The success of the song led to Buddy becoming involved with Ray Stevens — not only as a writer of several of Ray's other hit songs (*Sitting Up With The Dead, Power Tools,* and *Night Games*), but also as a script writer of, and actor in, several of Ray's hugely successful videos, as well as his first full-length movie, *Get Serious*.

Buddy, a versatile and accomplished writer, can best describe himself how *Mississippi Squirrel Revival* has affected his and his family's life. He writes:

> Several years ago, I heard about a young man who was paying his way through seminary by working in a butcher shop. On his first day at work, a woman who was a regular customer asked if he was going to be the new butcher. He told her that he was just there working while he went to school. "And what are you going to school to learn to be?" she asked. When he proudly replied, "I am going to learn to be a preacher!" the lady laughed out loud and said, "Child,

you can't learn to be no preacher . . . either you is a preacher or you ain't!"

It's the same way with being a songwriter; either you is or you ain't. The young preacher was going to school to receive certification (to get his credentials in order), but songwriters have no place to go except the world around us. We learn early on that we are songwriters and then spend most of our lives looking for validation from ever-widening circles of humanity.

First our family, then our friends, and then our friends' friends, are the people who come to hear us sing and play songs. What we are looking for is that ultimate validation: A HIT. For a writer, HIT is an acronym for an Historically Important Tune. For Jimmy Dean it was *Big Bad John*; for Ray Stevens it was *Ahab the Arab*; for me it was *Mississippi Squirrel Revival*.

Hits are life changers. They say to the world that "this person is a songwriter," and they allow the writer to say deep down inside, "I knew I could do it."

My earliest recollection of writing was on my granddaddy's front porch when I was about four years old. He was sitting with some friends and asked me to sing them all the songs I had written. It was some nonsense that came out different every time I sang it to the tune of Hoagy Carmichael's *Stardust*, but they loved it. I loved the attention and kept on doing it for forty years.

During that time, I wrote over 500 songs, had over 30 recorded, a dozen charted, and a couple in the top 40. We kid ourselves sometimes and call these "hits," but they aren't. A hit is a song people talk about—and not just a whistle or a hum. A hit is a song people remember for years. Forty years, five hundred songs, and no hits? This is not unusual in the music business.

*Buddy and Carlene Kalb receiving their awards for
"Mississippi Squirrel Revival."*

My first hit came when I started to focus. I had been
encouraging Ray Stevens to record more comedy
songs. It was during a time in his career when he had
been moving in another direction—and given his tal-
ent, he could move in any direction he wanted. But I
was one of his friends, and I missed his comedy because he's simply the best at it that I've ever heard.

So, one day, I'm once again making my "Why
don't you do more comedy?" speech when he says,
"Look, if you want me to record comedy songs, then
why don't you write some comedy songs?!"

It's not easy . . . writing comedy songs. Most of
them come out silly, not funny. But I focused. For
months, all I tried to write were funny songs, and, boy,

did I turn out some junk. Then one day I was driving the family to Florida to visit my folks who had recently retired and moved there. We drove from Kansas City to Atlanta the first day, and got up early on the second day to make it in to Leesburg at a "decent hour." My wife Carlene and our three children had all gotten up earlier than they wanted and had a drive-thru fast-food breakfast in Macon, Georgia. By the time we hit Perry, they were all sound asleep. They slept and I drove. I tried to write—tumbling ideas over in my mind, thinking of funny situations. Then, on I-75 south, while passing a rest area just north of Cordele, Georgia, I saw a complete event in my mind. I mean I saw it all . . . the little church, the kids, the squirrel, Sister Bertha, the deacons, Harv Newlan, the whole thing. "Bam!" Just like that.

When Carlene woke up, I told her about it, and she laughed out loud. So, over the next two weeks, Carlene and I crafted the event into a story, and into a song.

Ray recorded the song, and MCA Records didn't think it was a hit. But a hit will not be denied. A rock station in Jackson, Mississippi, and a country station in Chicago started playing it, and pretty soon Paul Harvey was talking about it on his radio show. Ray Stevens' comedy album started selling like hot cakes, eventually going platinum.

A couple of years later the real validation came. Carlene and I were in a pub in a small town in the British countryside when a woman asked us where we were from. When we replied, "Nashville," she said, "Oh, yes, where they play that country music and that delightful song about the squirrel that got loose in church and caused such havoc." Carlene and I smiled and said, "Yes, Ma'am, that's the place!"

Harlan Howard, a truly great songwriter, once told me that there were fewer than 400 people in America who make their living exclusively as songwriters. That's a small club. But thanks to my friend Ray Stevens, and a little Mississippi squirrel, both Carlene and I are members. And joining that club was one of the biggest changes in our lives . . . so far.

Heart of America Bone Marrow Registry
2124 East Meyer Boulevard
Kansas City, Missouri 64132-1183

Daddy's Hands

Holly Dunn

SONGWRITER:
Holly Dunn

I remember Daddy's hands folded silently in prayer,
And reaching out to hold me when I had a
nightmare.
You could read quite a story in the calluses and
lines,
Years of work and worry had left their mark
behind.

I remember Daddy's hand how they held my mom-
ma tight,
And patted my back for something done right.
There are things that I've forgotten that I loved
about the man,
But I'll always remember the love in Daddy's
hands.

> *Chorus:*
> *Daddy's hands were soft and kind when I was*
> *crying.*
> *Daddy's hands were hard as steel when I'd done*
> *wrong.*
> *Daddy's hands weren't always gentle but I've*
> *come to understand:*
> *There was always love in Daddy's hands.*

I remember Daddy's hands working till they bled,
Sacrificed to keep us all fed.
If I could do things over I'd live my life again,
And never take for granted the love in
Daddy's hands.

In his hit record, *You Never Even Call Me by My Name*, David Allan Coe claimed the perfect country song had to have the following ingredients: drinking, prison, trains, trucks. . . and mama.

It is indeed true that "mamas" have been written and sung about since the early days of country music. Merle Haggard's *Mama Tried*; Waylon and Willie's *Mamas Don't Let Your Babies Grow Up to Be Cowboys*; and C. W. McCall's *Roses for Mama* continued this trend in modern country songs.

But until Holly Dunn penned and recorded her classic, *Daddy's Hands*, there had been few songs about a father's love. Perhaps it was due to the fact that there were few female country artists until the 1970s, and male artists were reluctant to express their feelings for their fathers. Maybe it was the advent of the working mother, which forced more fathers to share in childrearing duties, which led to the demand for "daddy" songs. Whatever the reasons, with the release of *Daddy's Hands*, Holly Dunn struck a chord that has since caused "daddy" to become almost as common a theme as "mama."

Holly relates how the song came about:

> One morning in April of 1983, I woke up with the image of my dad's hands on my mind. As I got dressed that morning to go into my songwriting job down on Music Row, the image became so strong that I had to stop what I was doing, put down my make-up, pick up my guitar and write.

How could I have known that when I finished putting down my thoughts and feelings that day, that I would have written an anthem to a father's love and devotion that would be so far reaching. For me, it was simply something I needed to say to my dad. A catharsis of sorts, that had, in a way, taken me all of my life to articulate. And what a wonderful serendipity for me that the song that would become my "career record" and the springboard to my future successes, would be one written from pure, genuine emotion and not something contrived for the sole purpose of garnering radio airplay.

Daddy's Hands—the song and the real life subject, remain for me a true blessing in my life. The fact that it has meant so much to so many, leaves me with a feeling of awe and gratitude. That in a business fraught with selfish and self-serving goals—maybe, just maybe, I did something that really had value, something that really mattered . . .

One of the people whom *Daddy's Hands* really mattered to was a working woman in a field traditionally known for its "old boy network."

Country radio stations as employers have been slow to recognize the abilities of the female work force. Only in recent years have female radio personalities broken into the market, and still there are very few who are anchoring morning and drive-time slots. There are even fewer women who are given the responsibilities of programming—choosing what music is played on country stations. One of the few is Robynn Jaymes, a 33-year-old assistant programming director/music director for station WYYD in Lynchburg, Virginia. WYYD is the top-rated station in the region, in large part due to Robynn's significant contributions. She was named Medium Market Music Director of the Year by Gavin magazine in 1994.

Originally, Robynn had decided on a career in television. However, those plans did not pan out, so Robynn turned to radio as a viable alternative, and pursued it with a passion. In fact, she applied to every radio station in Lynchburg three times before one decided to give her a chance.

One of her main sources of inspiration and encouragement in her pursuit of a radio career came from her father, Robert Leggett. Though he had made his living in a more traditional occupation as a lawyer, he understood his daughter's attraction to "show business." When he was a law student, he had even done some television work, as well as talk radio, hosting a show which dealt with legal advice.

Robynn's dad became her mentor in many ways as she started her career with a part-time radio personality slot on WYYD and worked her way up to the afternoon drive position. Each week she would place a call to him at his Cincinnati office to ask his advice on any difficulties and obstacles she had encountered in her work. He was always a good sounding board in her decision-making process, as she rose to become one of the few female music directors at a major market radio station. He never wavered in his support of his only child, as she rose to success in this male-dominated industry.

Robynn talked on the air about the special relationship she had with her father. She often dedicated songs to her dad, and called him while on the air on special occasions, or just to chat. Her listeners came to know "Daddy" as he became a regular guest on Robynn's show.

July 7, 1994, was a day which should have been one of those special occasions, for it was her dad's birthday. That day Robynn received a call from him. His doctor had called him earlier that day to tell him he had three brain tumors and that his situation was terminal.

He had battled cancer for three years and beaten it twice in that period. Robynn had shared her father's battle with her listeners. *Daddy's Hands* became "their" song. Her audience had responded with prayers and thoughts which provided comfort and support to Robynn and her father.

When she received the call from her father, Robynn knew she must pass the news along to her "extended family" — her listening audience.

During the next six weeks, Robynn traveled to Cincinnati frequently in order to be at her father's side. She had recently been appointed to the prestigious position of Agenda Committee Chairwoman for the Country Radio Seminar (the most important gathering of people in the radio industry, held annually in Nashville). It was an honor which brought with it a great deal of responsibility. Robynn thought about resigning the position due to her father's illness, but he would hear none of that. He insisted that Robynn continue. He told her she had worked for years to achieve this well-deserved honor, and he did not want to see her give it up — even though it meant he would see her

*Robert Leggett and Robynn Jaymes at the
Opryland Hotel in March of '93.*

less in his last days. Unfortunately, these days
came all too quickly.

On August 30, 1994, Robynn received word
from her mother that her father had slipped into a
coma. Robynn and her nephew made the drive
from Virginia to Cincinnati, arriving at 1:30 a.m.
Her mother had just received news from the doctors that her father was not expected to make it
through the night. Robynn went to be with him.

Robynn tells about the last hours she spent
with her father: "I don't really know what I said to

him, but I talked a lot. I wanted him to know I was there . . . and I was when he took his last breath."

As he had been there for her all of her life, Robynn was there for her daddy to hold his hand in his final moments of life.

The next day, Robynn informed her co-workers back at the station of what had happened. Scott Walker was filling in for Robynn on her afternoon shift when he told her listeners about her father's death. They responded as though they too had lost a family member. Over 600 cards and flower arrangements were sent by listeners to the funeral home handling the arrangements for Mr. Leggett's service. After the beautiful ceremony ended, Robynn, her mom, her sister, and her niece got into the car for the ride to the cemetery.

Robynn shares what happened next: "Country music is so much a part of our family that we had the radio softly playing in the background. It was then and there that *Daddy's Hands* came on WUBE (a country station in Cincinnati). Through our tears, we smiled and sang along. We knew it was Dad's way of letting us know he was still with us . . . in our hearts."

Several months after her father passed away, Robynn was asked to speak to a gathering of radio industry executives at St. Jude's Children's Research Hospital in Memphis, TN. One of WYYD's biggest community events is the annual radiothon which benefits the hospital. The hospital had asked Robynn to share with other radio stations how to have a successful event of this type in their area.

On the morning Robynn was to speak, as she was getting dressed, she began to talk aloud to her father as she had done often since his death. She told him that she would really like to say something about him in her speech, but she wasn't sure how to work it into her topic.

The radio was on in her hotel room, and once again her father "sent" her a message: *Daddy's Hands* began playing. Robynn smiled and said, "OK, I'll talk about ya, Dad!"

The reaction to her speech was emotional and overwhelming. Her work with St. Jude's continues today. Robynn says it's her "way of doing something in hopes that St. Jude's will ultimately find a cure for the disease that took my father's life."

In March of 1995, Robynn had the chance to share her story with Holly Dunn. Robynn relates that Holly was "very gracious and receptive. I just wanted her to know that her song had taken on a life she had never known about." Holly later presented Robynn with a lithograph copy of the lyrics of *Daddy's Hands*. Robynn had it framed with a picture of her dad.

Robynn still plays songs and dedicates them to her father, the man who supported and inspired his "little girl" in her career, as well as in life.

Though she can no longer reach out and touch them, Robynn will *always remember the love in daddy's hands*. And she knows that they still hold her and guide her even now as she continues to do what she loves best: "find a great song . . . and share it with 120,000 friends."

St. Jude's Children's Research Hospital
1 St. Jude Place
P.O. Box 3704
Memphis, Tennessee 38173-0704
(901)522-9733

Independance Day

Martina McBride

SONGWRITER:
Gretchen Peters

Well she seemed all right by dawn's early light
Though she looked a little worried and weak
She tried to pretend he wasn't drinkin' again
But Daddy'd left the proof on her cheek
And I was only eight years old that summer
I always seemed to be in the way
So I took myself down to the fair in town
On Independence Day

Well word gets around in a small, small town
They said he was a dangerous man
Mama was proud and she stood her ground
But she knew she was on the losin' end
Some folks whispered and some just talked
But everybody looked the other way
And when time ran out there was no one about
On Independence Day

> *Chorus:*
> *Let freedom ring, let the white dove sing*
> *Let the whole world know that today is a day*
>   *of reckoning*
> *Let the weak be strong, let the right be wrong*
> *Roll the stone away, let the guilty pay, it's*
>   *Independence Day*

Well she lit up the sky that fourth of July
By the time that the firemen came
They just put out the flames, took down some names
And sent me to the county home
Oh and I ain't sayin' it's right or it's wrong
But maybe it's the only way
Talk about your revolution
It's Independence Day

Repeat Chorus

Gretchen Peters is the writer of one of the most passionate "statement" songs ever written, *Independence Day*. The song was voted the CMA Song of the Year in 1995. Gretchen says the first question most people ask is, "Did you write this song from personal experience?" Fortunately, Gretchen had no personal experience with domestic abuse, which is the topic of the song. She does, however, relate that she has a "personal sense of outrage that it exists." Still, she never had any idea that one day she would sit down and write a song about the subject. She now feels that the subject chose her, rather than vice versa.

"I was there when the chorus came ringing into my head. For awhile, I didn't know what the chorus lyric meant, the 'white dove/day of reckoning' bit, so I just waited around for it to become clear to me. I struggled with *Independence Day* for almost two years, picking it up and putting it away again. It seemed so dark and bleak. I tried ending the story various ways, but it just didn't seem to want to end any other way than the way it does. So, after fighting it for awhile, I just listened to the song, and it told me. Only later did the irony of it dawn on me — that the woman in the song was looking for any other way to end it too."

Gretchen recorded the demo (the songwriter's version of the song, which is then pitched to artists) knowing that it would be a difficult song to get recorded. It was a strong statement and potentially too controversial for the conservative country radio market. Still, she felt that it was a worthwhile song and wanted it to be "out there in the world."

When the demo was completed, Gretchen followed the usual procedure of playing it for her publisher, Paul Worley. Contrary to what Gretchen thought his reaction would be, Paul loved it. In addition to being Gretchen's publisher, he also worked as Martina McBride's producer. In fact, he was looking for songs for McBride's second album. Paul played *Independence Day* for Martina, and she shared his enthusiasm for the song. She recorded it, and it became a hit single on her breakthrough platinum album, *The Way That I Am*.

Independence Day's climb through the charts did not occur without leaving some controversy in its wake. Some radio stations chose not to play the song. They felt that it was not appropriate subject matter, and they also frowned on the fact that it lacked a happy, or at least, a hopeful ending.

Fortunately, most stations chose to play the song. Once they did, the grass-roots reaction was phenomenal. Letters poured in to Martina McBride, as well as to Gretchen Peters. They heard from victims of domestic violence and those whose lives had been affected by this terrible abuse. One of the most powerful letters came from an attorney in Moscow, Idaho, named Craig Mosman. In September of 1993, Craig was asked to represent a Native American woman named Patty Gallagher. She had been accused of murdering her abusive husband as he slept.

The first trial ended with a hung jury, 11-1 for

acquittal. As the second trial began in Bonners Ferry, Idaho, Patty and Craig knew they were in for a difficult fight.

According to reports by Carolynn Farley, staff writer for the *Bonners Ferry Herald*, Patty had first met her husband Jim on a weekend visit to her mother's home in Portland, Oregon. When they began their relationship, she thought he was "nice and fun to be around."

Soon, Jim moved to Boise, Idaho, to be with her; and there his violent nature became apparent. Once, when Patty was trying to wake him up, he had struck her in the face with his fist because, he said, "she scared him."

On another occasion, she was awakened by Jim holding the back of her head as he brandished a knife at her throat. He told her he had been having a nightmare about his ex-wife, Irene Swenson. During the second trial, Ms. Swenson testified that in the course of their 16-year marriage, Jim had beaten her with a bullwhip, and had once put a gun to her head and pulled the trigger. She also stated that on one occasion, when she had tried to leave him while she was eight-and-a-half months pregnant, Jim had threatened to cut her unborn child out of her womb with a hunting knife. He told her she could leave, but he refused to allow her to take his child with her.

Kathy Elliot, his 30-year-old daughter from a previous marriage, testified that her dad had attached wires to her toes and sent electricity through her body when she wet her pants as a child. She also told of being tossed into a freezing lake by her father for forgetting to put the lid on the garbage can.

Jim Gallagher was a troubled man when Patty married him. His violent episodes increased in frequency during their 16-year relationship. He regularly beat their sons, Nath and Zeb, with a rubber hose and a stick with surgical tubing nailed to the end. Zeb, the younger son, who was 13 at the time of the trial, testified that his father built a "torture chamber" in his shop. Inside the shed, he attached handcuffs to a rope and used the device to hoist the boys off the ground to whip them. It is difficult to imagine what offense could possibly have been bad enough for a father to "punish" his son in such a manner. Once, he chained Nath, 15 at the time of the proceedings, inside the shed after he had accidentally spilled his breakfast cereal. A witness testified that, another time, Jim disciplined Nath for biting the witness's son. Jim picked Nath up and bit him hard enough to leave bruises all over his upper torso. "He said 'if Nath acted like a dog, he would be treated like a dog'."

The years of suffering this horrible treatment had taken their toll on Patty, Nath, and Zeb. They had lived in terror, and the violence had escalated with each passing year. The mental abuse was often as sadistic as the physical abuse. Patty testified that Jim once shot the family cat and a neighbor's cow. Jim also killed a nest of young blue jays while the family was feeding them, and hung the dead birds on the door to Patty's sewing room. Jim Gallagher allegedly raped his own wife, as well as his ex-wife. Irene Swenson testified that the rapes happened on several occasions during their relationship. He forced himself on Patty Gallagher after surgery. She told the court that the incident had caused her to hemorrhage, and forced her to return to the hospital for two weeks.

Patty and her family had attempted to flee before with disastrous results. The beatings intensified, and she and her boys were promised at gunpoint that they would never leave alive again.

Finally, it all came to an end on September 18, 1993. Jim Gallagher died at age 52 from a gunshot wound to the head. Patty was charged with first degree murder.

Despite all of the documented abuse, the first trial had ended in a hung jury. How was attorney Craig Mosman going to persuade a new jury to come to a unanimous decision to acquit Patty Gallagher? And how was Patty going to hold up through another grueling trial?

Craig found the answer to both questions one day as he was making the three-hour drive from his home in Moscow to Bonners Ferry where the month-long trial was being held. Although Craig was not an ardent country music fan, as he was scanning his radio dial, he happened to hear *Independence Day*. As Craig now relates, "It seemed like the message in the song was exactly what Patty Gallagher had been going through."

Craig purchased the Martina McBride CD and played it for Patty. The song touched Patty deeply, for she was at a point in her life where she doubted that anyone could understand the violence she had suffered. *Independence Day* became an anthem for her defense.

As the trial progressed, Lenore Walker, who

Patty Gallagher outside of courthouse during her trial.

was an expert on Battered Woman Syndrome, testified that it was her opinion that Patty Gallagher suffered from the syndrome. She stated that, if Patty had indeed shot her husband, "a battered woman in those circumstances would perceive that her only way to end the abuse was to use a gun." Ms. Walker also claimed, "A battered woman's intent is to stop herself and her loved ones from being hurt. The intent is to protect, not to kill."

County Prosecutor Randy Day urged the jury to forget prejudices and look at the facts when making their decision. "Our sympathy for Patricia Gallagher cannot be substituted for the rule of the law," he argued. Day said the facts were that Jim Gallagher was dead, and his wife Patty had admitted to sheriff's deputies that she shot him on the night she was arrested. Day stated that Battered Woman Syndrome "is not a license to kill."

Craig Mosman knew that Patty's fate might be decided by his closing argument. "Jim Gallagher, through the years, has punished Patty enough. It is time to set her free," he said. He continued, "The violence was going to happen and the only question was who was going to die. . . the first step in treating a snake bite is to kill the snake."

Craig asked the jurors to send the message that abuse is not acceptable to batterers in Idaho by returning an innocent verdict.

He used some of the lyrics to the chorus of *Independence Day* to make his final point.

> Let freedom ring, let the white dove sing
> Let the whole world know that today is the day of
>   reckoning
> Let the weak be strong, let the right be wrong
> Roll the stone away, let the guilty pay,
> It's Independence Day

The jury found Patty Gallagher not guilty. One comment from a juror expressed the general feelings of the entire jury: "We agreed the deceased had declared war on his family, and in wartime you can sneak up on the enemy."

In his letter to Martina McBride, Craig Mosman wrote: "Your song, *Independence Day*, provided great inspiration for me and Patty Gallagher throughout this case." Patty made Martina a special gift after the trial. It was a ceremonial Native American shield. Though she has not yet been able to present it to Martina, she remains grateful for the strength her song supplied during a difficult time. As Craig Mosman said in his letter to Martina, "In a very real way, you had a part in finally setting this family free."

Peace At Home
95 Berkley Street
Suite 107
Boston, Massachusetts 02116

A Mansion On The Hill

Hank Williams

SONGWRITER:
Hank Williams
Fred Rose

Tonight down here in the valley
I'm lonesome and oh how I feel
As I sit here alone in my cabin
I can see your mansion on the hill
So you recall when we parted
The story to me you revealed
You said you could live without love Dear
In your loveless mansion on the hill

I've waited all through the years, Love
To give you a heart true and real
'Cause I know you're living in sorrow
In your loveless mansion on the hill
The light shines bright from your window
The trees stand so silent and still
I know you're alone with your pride, Dear
In your loveless mansion on the hill

Many would say that the most influential artist in the history of country music was a man who died at the age of 29 in 1953 after only a six-year career. Not only did he write and record dozens of songs which became country classics. His songs also became hits for many of the top pop artists of his day such as Tony Bennett, Rosemary Clooney, Teresa Brewer, and Jo Stafford. He was the first "superstar" in country music, and his name is as well known today as it was during his lifetime. In dying, he became a legend. There have been many who emulated his style — but there was only one Hank Williams.

His story has become part of country music lore. Born Hiram Williams on September 17, 1923, in Mt. Olive, Alabama, he was taught to play the guitar as a young boy by a black street singer named Rufe Hayne, known as "Tee-Tot" by the local citizens.

He was discovered by Fred Rose, a partner with Roy Acuff in Acuff/Rose Music, one of Nashville's first publishing companies. Rose took charge of Hank's career, and by 1947 he had his first top-ten hit with *Move It On Over*. In 1949, Hank's recording of his own *Lovesick Blues* became his first #1 record, selling nearly 3,000,000 copies. He was invited to join the Grand Ole Opry; and during the next three years, he became a national phenomenon.

But Hank Williams not only wrote and sang sad songs, he lived them. In 1952, he and his wife Audrey divorced. Though Audrey had been the love of his life and the inspiration for many of his songs, their relationship had been volatile. It may be debated by his biographers whether or not his problems with Audrey led to his problems with alcohol. But one thing is true: after their divorce, Hank went down fast.

He was dismissed from the Opry later that same year. Though he remarried in October of 1952, the time he shared with his new wife, Billie Jean Eshliman, was short lived. Less than three months later, Hank Williams died in the back seat of his Cadillac en route to a New Year's Day show in Canton, Ohio. His death was attributed to a fatal combination of alcohol and chloral hydrate; but many will always believe that he died of the broken heart he sang and wrote about so often.

A young boy named Beecher O'Quinn, Jr., better known as Junior, was nine years old when Hank Williams passed away. He remembers the day well. But it was not until five years later on New Year's Day in 1958 that the impact of Hank Williams' life, death, and music made its mark on young Junior.

A disc jockey named Curly White was hosting what had become an annual New Year's Day tradition on country radio stations across the nation—a Hank Williams tribute. Junior was sitting in the front seat of his older brother's 1948 Chevrolet when he was struck by the mournful music coming from the radio. As he now recalls:

"The song that really grabbed my attention was *Mansion on the Hill*. I thought it was the most beautiful song that I had ever heard—the music, the voice, and the words seemed to go together perfectly. *Mansion on the Hill* is still my all-time favorite Hank Williams song. The radio tribute lasted around two hours. I almost ran my brother's car battery down — and the more I listened, the more fascinated I became. At that time, of course, I didn't even know what Hank looked like, as I had never seen a picture of him. From the sincerity in his voice, however, I thought he sounded like a man in his late forties or early fifties. Later, I was surprised to learn that he was just a little more than 29 years of age at the time of his death."

Junior began to collect Hank Williams records and played them on the small record player he shared with his two younger sisters. His grandmother eventually helped him buy his own record player, and he increased his collection of Hank Williams music to more than 29 extended-play albums. He also began collecting pictures, stories, magazine articles, books, and virtually anything he could find about Hank. As he grew up and his life went on, Junior continued to be a big fan of Hank Williams, Sr.

But in November of 1990, Junior became more than just another fan. He began a campaign that will forever stand as a tribute to this legendary performer.

As Junior was checking his mail at the post office one morning, he noticed a clipboard containing information about the different commemorative stamps the postal service had begun to issue. He saw the various themes and people that were due to appear on upcoming stamps, and thought to

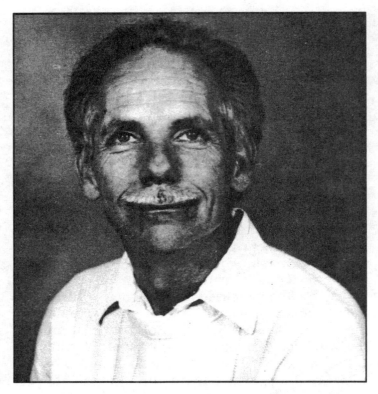

Beecher O'Quinn, Jr.

himself that if anybody deserved such an honor, it was Hank Williams.

He went home that night and couldn't sleep from thinking about his idea. He had no knowledge of how to initiate such a project, but by the next day he had decided that it was his mission. (At that time he also had no knowledge that a decade earlier a group of fans had tried unsuccessfully to accomplish the same task).

Junior checked with the local postmaster and was given the address of the Citizens Stamp Advisory Committee in Washington, D.C. The next day he wrote a letter to the committee and placed Hank's name in nomination.

Junior didn't stop there. He also went to the library and looked up the names and addresses of various governors, U.S. congressmen, and senators. He sent them all letters asking for their support in his effort.

In addition, he wrote Merle Kilgore, Hank Williams, Jr.'s, manager, to receive their blessing on the project. After Merle and Hank, Jr., received assurances that Junior's motives for pursuing this project were out of a great love and respect for Hank, Sr., they supported him wholeheartedly.

Junior enlisted the support of his friend Teddy Bradshaw, who became in essence the "press agent" for this endeavor. Teddy began setting up interviews for television, radio, and newspapers. As the word spread about the drive to see Hank's stamp become a reality, the momentum increased like a snowball rolling down a hill. A petition drive was launched, and offers of help from people all over the country poured in. One woman in California, Cathy Malfatti, sent out over 2,000 letters to other political leaders in her part of the country, as well as to newspapers and periodicals.

Before it was over, some 7,000 pieces of mail had been sent out. Junior ended up receiving the support of 22 governors (including then-Arkansas governor Bill Clinton), 10 U.S. senators, 8 U.S. representatives, and 28 mayors. With the help of many people, he was able to get the signatures of a host of country stars on his petitions, including Charlie Pride (who also wrote a letter of support), Ray Price, Boxcar Willie, Kitty Wells, Mel Tillis, Mickey Gilley, the Oak Ridge Boys, Minnie Pearl . . . and the list goes on and on.

Junior was, in fact, informed that the postal service got more letters about Hank's stamp than they received for the highly publicized Elvis commemorative stamp.

Nearly three years passed as Junior O'Quinn continued working on the project. Finally, at country music's Fan Fair on June 9, 1993, his dream became a reality. Marvin Runyon, the Postmaster General of the United States, along with Hank Williams, Jr., unveiled the Hank Williams, Sr., Commemorative Postage Stamp on the stage in front of thousands of Fan Fair attendees.

Junior O'Quinn stood and watched with pride — not because of something he had accomplished, but because the accomplishments of his hero were finally being recognized.

Because of the success of the commemorative stamp, Junior has participated in many other events that honor the memory of Hank Williams and his music. He even helped organize the Hank Williams, Sr., International Society and Fan Club. But his experiences in organizing the drive for Hank's stamp will probably always remain his biggest thrill. As Junior now says:

"I sincerely feel the stamp is a great tribute and national honor for a man who I consider to be one of the greatest singers and songwriters of all time. I

The Hank Williams Commemorative Stamp

don't think there is anybody that Hank Williams can be compared with. He was one of a kind."

And that nine-year-old boy, who first heard *Mansion on the Hill* back in 1958, became a one-of-a-kind fan whose dedication will help to forever keep alive the legacy of his idol — Hank Williams, Sr.

If you'd like to join the Hank Williams, Sr., Fan Club, please write to:
The Hank Williams, Sr., International Society & Fan Club
c/o Mary H. Wallace
P.O. Box 280
Georgiana, Alabama 36033

Is There Life Out There

Reba McEntire

SONGWRITER:
Susan Longacre
Rick Giles

She married when she was twenty
She thought she was ready
Now she's not so sure
She thought she'd done some living
But now she's just wonderin'
What she's living for
Now she's feeling that there's something more

Chorus:
Is there life out there
So much she hasn't done
Is there life beyond
Her family and her home
She's done what she should
Should she do what she dare
She doesn't want to leave
She's just wonderin'
Is there life out there

She's always lived for tomorrow
She's never learned how
To live for today
She's dyin' to try something foolish
Do something crazy
Or just get away
Something for herself for a change

Repeat Chorus

There's a place in the sun that she's never been
Where life is fair and time is a friend
Would she do it the same as she did back then
She looks out the window and wonders again

Repeat Chorus

The song *Is There Life Out There* was released in 1991. It was yet another hit, in a decade-and-a-half string of hits, for country music superstar Reba McEntire. But perhaps no other song Reba has ever recorded has had a more positive influence on her audience than this Rick Giles/Susan Longacre composition.

The lyrics of the song tell the story of a woman who married when she was 20, and now is going through a stage of questioning the direction her life has taken. She is not particularly unhappy with her life. As she states in the song, *she doesn't want to leave,* but still she is unfulfilled.

Reba McEntire has always been a recording artist with a strong following of women, perhaps because she is a strong woman who is not afraid to make a statement. The statement she wanted to make with *Is There Life Out There* was enhanced by the video of the song, directed by Jack Cole.

In the video, Reba plays the part of Maggie O'Connor—a waitress, wife, and the mother of two young children. Maggie has gone back to college to get her degree, and the video depicts the trials and tribulations this working mother must endure in pursuit of her dream. At the end of the piece, she is shown walking down the aisle to receive her diploma and being applauded by the crowd, including her family (the part of the husband was played by pop singer Huey Lewis).

Though the song's lyrics had not included this story line, the video's treatment inspired thousands of working mothers to go back to school to try to achieve the goal of earning their degree, just as Maggie O'Connor did in the video.

But for Candy Winnett of Twin Falls, Idaho, seeing the video was like watching her own life. She was already chasing the distant dream of getting her college education while trying to raise two children. She had reached a crossroads and the roadblocks that stood in her way had almost caused her to give up her dream.

In May of 1987, Candy had graduated from high school and gotten married shortly thereafter. The man she married was nine years older, and Candy was pregnant with his baby. Her family did not approve of the marriage.

It only added to the conflict she was already experiencing at home. Because of the situation going on at home, her parents chose not to attend her graduation.

In November of the same year, Candy gave birth to her first child, a beautiful baby girl named Shaneal. Unfortunately, the joy of the event was not enough to repair the increasingly rocky marriage. Within a year, Candy found herself divorced and a single mother.

She decided to enroll in a computerized bookkeeping course at the College of Southern Idaho, hoping to gain her Associate's Degree in two years. By the end of those two years, Candy had remarried, taken two jobs, and her daughter Shaneal had become a toddler. It was very difficult to find the time to take more than a couple of night classes each semester. Her dream remained so far away.

Her counselor at the college suggested she

needed to set some priorities if she ever were going to finish school. Determined, Candy got a new job working at a convenience store on the swing shift and every weekend, which enabled her to become a full-time student.

Her new marriage began to suffer as her husband worked days and she worked evenings. They saw each other less and less. Candy would come home from work at 11:00 p.m., stay up till 1:00 a.m. studying, and then be back up at 5:00 a.m. to care for Shaneal. As she was finishing up that semester, Candy got some unexpected news: she was pregnant again.

The pregnancy was difficult. Five months into it, Candy went into pre-term labor and was told she would have to spend the remaining four months of her pregnancy on medication and confined to her bed. Not only would she have to quit her job, but she would miss the summer and fall semesters at the college. Once again, her dream would have to be put on hold.

One day as she lay on the couch, during this period of forced inactivity, Candy saw Reba's video of *Is There Life Out There*. It didn't just hit home, it hit her heart. Candy now recalls:

"As the lyrics rang out, I could hear her singing my thoughts and my heartfelt yearnings. Every part of the video seemed to speak to me, about me. It mirrored my life, my hopes, my fears. *There's a place in the sun that she's never been; where life is fair and time is her friend. Would she do it the same as she did back then?*

"The song made me think. Would I do it the same? Would I have married my first husband?

Candy Winnett and Reba McEntire

Would I have moved out of the house so young, instead of going to college right away? It sure would have been easier. I, too, didn't need *any more accidents in my life*. The only thing I knew for sure was that I had a family that I loved, and I had a dream. And somehow those two things had to come together. I didn't want to leave, either. But there was life out there, and I was determined to get my fair share of it. I was going to graduate. That was going to be my place in the sun."

Eight months after Candy's son, Brandon, was born, she again enrolled in school. She signed up for a full load of 18 credits and soon made the Dean's List and Honor Roll.

But even as she got her dream back on track, there were still some rough times ahead. As Candy now relates:

"My husband would complain that if I wasn't at school or work, I had my head buried in a textbook. So, I tried to accommodate everyone. At first, I tried to put my homework off until after the kids were in bed, but that took away from any private time with my husband. So then I tried to involve the kids in what I was doing. Shaneal and I would camp out on the floor in a pile of books and papers, she with her crayons, and I with my adding machine and notes. One time she got a little carried away with the crayons and scribbled all over a home quiz I was supposed to hand in the next morning. My first reaction was absolute misery. Then I remembered the stains on Reba's term paper. *I learned more from the stains than I did the paper.* Well, the teacher wasn't quite so understanding and I didn't get the 'A' I thought I had earned. But Shaneal and I did have a great time. Spending time as a family and pouring my heart and soul into school didn't always mesh. I didn't want to just slide through school, barely passing. Eventually, it got to be too much. I wanted more and felt like I could achieve it. Unfortunately, my husband didn't want more. He wanted his family. After four years together and one semester left toward getting my degree, we separated."

In February of 1994, Candy started a new job as a secretary/bookkeeper for an engineering firm. She also forcefully attacked the last semester of school that stood between her and her degree. At times, she didn't feel as though she could stand the stress of a full-time job, school, and raising two children alone. Whenever she felt that way, she would go out and sit in her car, punch in her Reba tape, and sing *Is There*

Life Out There at the top of her lungs. After playing the song over and over, Candy could go back into the house and face life again.

In April of that year, she was chosen by the college to go to a state competition of a club she had joined called Business Professionals of America. She placed second in the state of Idaho in the field of payroll accounting. In May, she was sent by the school to a national competition in San Francisco, where she placed in the top ten in the nation in the same field.

On Friday, May 13, 1994, Candy Winnett's dream finally came true as she graduated with her Associate of Applied Science degree in Computerized Bookkeeping, with a cumulative grade point average of 3.42. As she walked across the stage to get her diploma, she couldn't help thinking about Reba's portrayal of Maggie O'Connor — for out in the crowd her mother, her two brothers, her two children, and. . . her ex-husband Cory stood and cheered. She had reached her place in the sun and this time her family was there. She had worked hard and made them proud; she had earned it.

The story could have ended happily there, but the icing on the cake was still to come.

Six days after Candy graduated from college, she got a phone call from Vicki Miceli, a woman who worked for a television program called EXTRA. Ms. Miceli was calling Candy to see if she would be interested in doing an interview for their program with Reba McEntire, as she was filming the movie based on the video of *Is There Life Out There*. They had heard about Candy's story through Reba's management company, Starstruck Entertainment. Candy's mom and older brother had written letters and made phone calls to Starstruck trying to get an autographed picture of Reba for Candy's graduation present. They told the folks at Starstruck how much the video resembled Candy's life.

A week after receiving the phone call from EXTRA, Candy was on the plane headed for Nashville. The only other time she had ever flown was when she had gone to the BPA competition in San Francisco. When Candy arrived in Nashville, she was met by Tracy Green, the field producer for EXTRA. Along with the camera crew, they drove to Louisville, where parts of the movie were being filmed.

Candy spent the morning on the set, and got to watch the making of the movie. Later that afternoon, she finally got the chance to sit and talk with Reba. They talked for ten minutes before it was time for filming to resume on the set.

As they sat on the porch of the house where the filming was taking place, Candy presented Reba with a bud vase containing two yellow roses as a token of her appreciation. She told Reba, "Thank you for helping me find my place in the sun." The whole set was quiet for this moving moment. Then Reba stood up, and with her characteristic spunk, said, "Give me a hug, I gotta get back to work!"

And so did Candy.

Fall of 1995 finds her starting school again. With the support and encouragement of the people she works with, Candy will pursue her second Associate of Applied Science degree.

Two working women, Reba McEntire and Candy Winnett, have found that "there is life out there" . . . and they continue to live it to the fullest.

Primary Children's Medical Center
100 N. Medical Drive
Salt Lake City, Utah 84113

Hell And High Water

T. Graham Brown

SONGWRITER:
T. Graham Brown
Alex Harvey

Now Baby don't worry—If he troubles your mind
It'll all wash away girl—In the river of time
If you need a shoulder—I'll be around
(Be) your rock to hold on to—Till the river
   goes down

> *Chorus:*
> *(Cause) it's hell and high water*
> *That you're goin through*
> *But come hell or high water*
> *I'll be here waiting for you*

I can't keep you from crying
I can't stop your pain
The brightest of sunshine
Never could stop the rain
But you know that I'll be there
Just like that old sun
I'll be your good morning
When your crying's all done

> *Repeat Chorus*

T. Graham Brown and Alex Harvey got together one morning in 1985 to write together for the first time. Alex invited T. to join him for breakfast. Following the meal, they began kicking around the phrase "come hell or high water" as an idea for a song. They decided to write the song as a tribute to their wives, Sheila Brown and Ava Harvey. With that inspiration, as T. now says, "The song just fell out of the sky." In only a matter of hours, they had it finished and were headed for the golf course. Prior to their golf game, they played the song for Alex's wife, Ava. As she began crying, T. and Alex shed a few tears themselves. They knew they had a hit.

T. Graham Brown went on to record the song for his debut album, *I Tell It Like It Used to Be*, and *Hell and High Water* became his first #1 song. It also established him as one of the top artists of the late 1980s.

At about the same time T. and Alex were celebrating their hit record, a young man in Austin, Texas, was celebrating his 22nd birthday with a few of his friends.

Robert Williams had recently moved to Austin. He was doing carpentry work, and as his mother Lynda now says, "just beginning to do things he wanted to do and see what life's about."

The night of his 22nd birthday, Robert and his friends were at a party. Across the street from where the party was being held, there was a tower that several of his buddies had climbed many times before. That night Robert decided to climb the tower for the first time. He was not aware that any high-voltage lines were close by.

As he was climbing the tower, Robert came into contact with one of the lines. It was carrying approximately 18,000 volts of electricity. He fell approximately 35 feet from the tower. His right leg was broken in three places, the femur bone on his left leg was broken, and his left hip was broken. Both hands were burned severely.

Thanks to the Austin EMS (Emergency Medical Service) and their quick response and knowledge, Robert was kept alive en-route to the hospital, though they almost lost him several times. The doctors at Breckenridge Hospital, where he was taken, worked feverishly to stabilize Robert.

At 2:00 a.m., his mother, Lynda Boaz, received a call from the doctors at Breckenridge. She was notified of Robert's condition. The doctor she spoke with informed Lynda that Robert would need to be moved to another facility to be treated. Lynda asked the doctor a question that any parent in such anguish would understand: "What would you do if he were your son?" The doctor immediately told Lynda that Brooks Burn Center in San Antonio would be the place he would send his son. Lynda agreed and Robert was life-flighted to Brooks.

Unfortunately, they were not able to save his right leg. Later in November, he also lost his right hand. The damage done when he was electrocuted had been too great. Still, Robert was left handed, and though his left hand was badly injured, he wanted desperately to keep it. Lynda conferred with the doctors and was told Robert would need to be transferred once again, this time to Wolford

Hall Hospital on the Lockland Air Force Base, where plastic surgeons could perform micro-surgery in order to try to save his left hand.

Lynda followed the ambulance to Wolford Hall. After Robert was checked in, she decided to return to Brooks Burn Center where she had spent the previous evening. Brooks was only a forty-minute drive, but as Lynda drove she could not help but think how much Robert might need her back at Wolford Hall. When she arrived at Brooks and got back to her room, she realized there was no way she could spend the night away from her son. Even though it was almost midnight, and a tremendous thunderstorm was raging, Lynda turned around and headed back on unfamiliar roads to Wolford Hall. Not only was she afraid of getting lost, but she was worried sick about Robert and wanted to be close to him.

As the rain poured down around her, Lynda began to pray for strength and guidance, hoping the highway on her way back would not be flooded from the heavy downpour. It was at this tense and fearful moment that Lynda heard a song for the first time which she now says, "God meant for me to hear." As the radio personality announced that he would next be playing T. Graham Brown's new single, *Hell and High Water*, Lynda thought to herself, "That is exactly what I am going through." In Lynda's words:

"The first line of the song, *Now, baby, don't worry*, immediately caught my attention, because that's what my daddy always used to say to me when I was upset about something. I realized then that this was a song God had sent me to help me through what I was experiencing. When it got to the chorus, and T. Graham sang, *It's hell and high water that you're going through*, it hit so close to my heart. And the second verse really said so much to me, because I knew I would not be able to keep Robert from crying or stop his pain. But I was determined to be there, *Just like that old sun, I'll be your good morning, when your crying's all done.* I sang those last two lines all the way back to the hospital, and kept repeating them, adding Robert's name to the song. I was going to be there when his crying was all done."

As Lynda was figuratively driving through the "high water," Robert was literally "going through hell." Though Robert had been sedated, the pain from his severe burns was intense. Early on, during this period of "hell," Robert experienced what now seems to have been a bit of "heaven." Robert describes his out-of-body experience:

"I floated up to the corner of the operating room, and when I looked down I could see myself lying on the table. I watched the doctors working on my body for a short time, but soon something or somebody came along and took me from the room. I never got a visual impression, just a feeling of this presence. I was taken back to my first home in Clute, Texas, where I was originally raised. Then I went to Austin where I had lived at the time of the accident. I saw people but they couldn't see me. I could hear them, but they never heard me, as I never said a word. The presence that was guiding me along never spoke either. I could only feel it pulling me. I still don't understand what it meant, but it was something I'll never forget."

Robert remained at Wolford Hall Hospital until the end of December and was transferred back to Brooks Burn Center. He remained at Brooks until January. His mom and his family were there by his side through it all. When he was released, Lynda and her husband Gene, Robert's step-father, brought him to their home to West Columbia. Robert's struggle was just beginning.

Robert had been very active all his life. He once had a .420 batting average in baseball, and had also been a champion skeet shooter. He had raced motorcycles and loved taking bicycles apart and putting them back together. He had always done things with his hands, and now he was without one of them. His legs had never failed him, and now he had lost one of them. Most people might have chosen to quit living and simply exist. Most people have neither a mother like Lynda Boaz, nor the will to live like Robert Williams.

Robert's former Little League baseball coach, Mr. Howard Hughes, wrote Robert a touching letter of encouragement. In the letter he said;

> I was always amazed how a little blond 10-year-old, with legs one-half as long as the other guys had, could move them twice as fast, thus outrunning all those long-legged boys. I thought about it a lot after your mom called. I was so honored that she went to all the trouble to run us down after all these years. My heart aches for you. I wish we could 'sop up' some of the hurt and pain that you are going through. I have asked my Heavenly Father that He give you comfort and strength, and to your Mom, Dad, Melinda, and Mike. This letter is extremely difficult for me to write.

It's hard enough knowing a young man I cared a lot about has had this unfortunate mishap. But it's difficult for another reason also; that is, I have such a vivid recollection of all your Astros and Padres games. As I said, I thought a lot about that, and the answer is Desire and Spirit. You've heard me say so many times that God gives us gifts in this life for a reason. He expects us to use them. Perhaps now I know why Robert Williams was given a double dose of Desire. I believe that now your gifts of Desire and Spirit may be used by you in a far more important way than just running the bases. I'm somewhat of a believer that God knows when we are born what things we are going to encounter in this life, you see. You are now being called upon to use that Desire and Competitive Spirit to overcome the challenge that's ahead of you by getting yourself well. I know with all your God-given gifts you won't let anything slow you down. I'm sending to you an old boxscore of an old Astros game 5/9/77, where R. Williams had a pretty good game. I have all that stuff still, it's priceless to an old man like me. We love you.

Robert moved in with Lynda and Gene as he began his rehabilitation and adjusted to the prosthesis' designed for him. And adjust he did. Though it was a long process, Robert worked diligently as he learned to operate his new arm and leg. He also had to relearn how to drive. He studied and was awarded his GED at home.

The struggle was hard for Lynda as well. It was not easy for her to watch her son endure this incredible adversity. She now says that, "Every time I needed comfort, it seemed like I would hear the

Robert Williams and T. Graham Brown

song, *Hell and High Water*, on the radio, and I found it." She was the rock that Robert held onto till the river went down.

Lynda told her friend Dorothy McGuire how *Hell and High Water* had helped her during Robert's hospitalization and rehabilitation. Dorothy suggested they write to T. Graham Brown's Fan Club and let them know how much the song had meant. She did, and T. named the family honorary members of the fan club.

When T. Graham came to Houston the following year, Linda, Gene, Robert, and Dorothy were able to go down to see his concert. Afterward, T.

invited them on the tour bus. They met T.'s band and spent a good deal of time sharing their story with T.

Later, Robert was able to meet T. again at the annual Great Mosquito Festival held in Clute, Texas. He says, "I had to fight my way through a crowd, but I got to him. I gave him a big kiss on the cheek."

Their relationship continues today. Robert calls T. Graham "a damn good fella," and T. says of Robert, "He's one courageous young man, and he's promised to take me fishin' someday." At Christmas, the families even exchange Christmas cards.

Robert will be 31 years old on his next birthday. He recently received a new prosthesis that he helped design. He is now living on his own, and works full time for his step-father at his construction company. Since he is only six miles from the ocean, Robert can pursue one of his favorite activities, fishing. He enjoys regular fish fries at the beach and his home. He says his mother Lynda, as well as Gene and the rest of his family, and many prayers from many people, are the reasons he is still alive today. Of Lynda, Robert says, "She was my partner through it all. She was there to push me and encourage me to go on with my life. She is one hell of a lady."

Lynda now says that it seems ironic that the accident happened on Robert's birthday. "On October 26, 1964, the Lord gave me Robert . . . and on October 26, 1986, He gave him back. People just don't understand the power of prayer. God works in mysterious ways."

As T. Graham Brown said, the song *Hell and*

High Water simply "fell out of the sky." For Lynda Boaz, Robert Williams, and millions of others whose lives it touched, God was at work.

Lynda Boaz & Robert Williams requested
that readers donate to their
local EMS (Emergency Medical Service).

The Last Verse

The letters from fans that we received for this book were filled with many interesting and poignant stories. Of course, because of the large number of letters we received, we could not include all of them. Some of the letters told the stories better than I ever could. For this final chapter, we are including excerpts from several of them.

My mother and I were avid fans of Alan Jackson.

Mama moved in with my family in August of 1993, after losing my father in March of that same year. My family, at the time of my mother's arrival, consisted of my husband, his daughter, Shelli, and my son, Bobby. Mama was extremely depressed after the loss of my dad. At the time of his death, she had been a diabetic for 37 years and had lost her left leg just below the knee. She depended on him for most everything. I had always promised Pop that I would take care of Mama.

Mama never tried to be difficult. As a matter of fact, she tried to help with everything she could. She was not a burden, only an invalid. Over a period of less than a year, the added responsibilities took their toll. Bobby and Shelli moved out (for reasons other than Grandma). Although the prior couple of years had been tough on both of them, they were grown and wanted to be on their own.

The week before they began moving, Mama had her right leg amputated above the knee. She had also been diagnosed as having congestive heart failure along with numerous other complications.

The day Bobby and Shelli started moving out, my husband of 10 years walked out on me. All of a sudden there were no children, no husband, and an even more dependent mother.

I didn't quite go off the deep end, but I came close. I brought Mama home to an empty house—which, to say the least, was not easy on her either. I'm not sure if she ever knew that I needed her as much, if not more, than she needed me at that point in time. She was the reason to continue.

Mama had a series of mini-strokes in September of 1994. This caused her to be partially paralyzed, and she lost her eyesight. One last wish Mama had was to meet Alan Jackson.

Although a meeting was never accomplished, Alan's office sent Mama an autographed picture and a video (neither of which she could see). The office also sent all of Alan's CDs. Mama and I sat here damn near every night from then until the end and listened to Alan sing.

Mama passed away March 18 (one year—364 days after my dad's death). Yes, over the past two and a half years, somehow, I've learned how to listen.

I played "Song for the Life" at Mama's funeral services. The song was a tribute to Mama since Alan was her favorite singer, but it was also for me. I feel she heard, and we both understood.

—Nita, Friendswood, Texas

I have been married for 29 years, and 10 years after I was married my husband became ill. We had three children by then. They were five, seven, and nine so I had to raise our three children by myself because my husband couldn't help very much. So for the last 19 years, I have raised my children up and taken care of a sick husband. And for the last four years, I've held down two full-time jobs.

I turned real bitter towards the world. These hospital bills will never get paid off.

They just keep piling up, and I have to pay on all of them every week or they will take my checks. I can't even afford to get a half-way decent car. My car goes when it feels like it. I was stranded last winter for two hours in a snowstorm with 28-below-zero temperatures. I just about froze to death.

I used to ask God, "Why me? What have I done so bad that for most of my life I have had to work for nothing?" My co-workers always ask me, "Where are you going on vacation?" I haven't done anything but work for so long, I wouldn't know what to do if I had the chance.

But my one goal is to meet the guy that changed my life. Billy Ray Cyrus made me look at life through his eyes. His song "Storm In The Heartland" changed my life completely around.

"They made it through the flood of '93
But this is gonna be the death of me.
I can't hide the tears of a desperate man."

It hit me—they made it. They shed their

tears, but they kept going on. And that's what I have to do.

What I learned from the song was that you can rise above anything if you believe. And when there's a "storm in the heartland" you can rise above it.

—Delores, Sheridan, Michigan

I was a twin born to parents who already had quite a few children. At birth, I was given away to live with my aunt and uncle. They had no small children and were unprepared for a newborn. I wore dishcloths for diapers and slept in a dresser drawer. They eventually got the things that they needed for a baby and from then on made sure that I had what I needed. They weren't well off, so we lived with just the basics.

My Aunt Mary taught me how to cook and clean, can food, sew, and a lot about plants and gardening. We enjoyed doing crossword puzzles and jigsaw puzzles and picking berries together. She was a great "mom," and a major influence in my life. When she was diagnosed for cancer on her lung, she didn't give up. I took her for chemotherapy and I did my best to take care of her. When she died, I just couldn't believe it. I was lost and scared and angry, and I lived life that way.

I go to see Patty Loveless in concert every chance I get. It wasn't until I heard her sing, "How Can I Help You Say Goodbye" that I was able to really say good-bye to my Aunt Mary. Although I miss my aunt very much, I now understand, and I go on with good memories.

—Joan, Lake Luzerne, New York

In 1982, I used to go to my neighborhood bar, and there I met a wonderful man. I met

Bob through his friends. They would play the jukebox, and Bob and I would dance.

In 1985 I was really sick with all kinds of symptoms. The doctors put me in the hospital. The third morning my doctor came in and told me I had MS. I had to have chemotherapy. Bob was there every day with me. I have never known that kind of love or commitment. After I was released from the hospital, not only did I gain weight, but my hair was falling out. But Bob was there through it all. Bob got me to the doctor's office. And he made me smile.

Bob, to me, is a very special man. He would do anything for me. It's hard in this day and age to find a man like Bob. These are some of the reasons "Forever and Ever Amen" is my favorite song for Mr. Bob and me. It seems that Bob and I lived through that song.

Bob and I have been together for 13 years and I will love his family "forever and ever amen!"

—Mary, Wapello, Iowa

 Hats off, many many thanks, and a very big "Yee Haw" to Alan Jackson, for his great recording of "Livin' on Love." From the very first moment that we heard this recording, we felt as though it was written "especially" for us!

 We are an elderly couple that very much loves country music, with Alan Jackson being our favorite artist.

 How very true are the words to this song, and it has inspired our lives greatly. Here we are, alone, with children gone, just depending on each other for love and support, but still hopelessly, very much in love! As the song says, "Without somebody, nothin' ain't worth a dime."

 We are very thankful to God for giving us a good marriage and giving us this togetherness. And we would like to add a very special thank-you to Alan Jackson, and all of his band members, for giving us so much hope, through his great music, that we can still continue to be "Livin' On Love" for many years to come.

—Elaine, Albuquerque, New Mexico

I never knew what the song "Angel Flying Too Close to the Ground" meant to me, and eventually my wife.

My drinking buddy and I listened to this song over and over until we wore out two cassettes.

Around this same period of time, we had some good friends, John and Sherry, whose son Matthew was diagnosed with neuro-blastoma cancer. At only three and a half years old, Matthew was very smart and special. I began sending him get-well cards every day, which he anxiously looked for in his mailbox. To bring him more mail, I solicited for people to write him through the Willie

Nelson Fan Club. Matthew began receiving cards from all over America and the world.

One of those people writing from overseas was Helen of Sydney, Australia. She sent Matthew cards and gifts in response to the Willie Nelson Fan Club. She later began corresponding with me also, and we became very close at a long distance.

Unfortunately, Matthew soon died, and blessed his parents with a beautiful and spiritual passing. My friend, Bobby, and I were pall bearers for Matthew. As we were passing the cemetery following the burial, Willie began singing "Angel Flying Too Close to the Ground" on the radio. Then we knew why this song had been so special.

Helen and I continued to write and talk on the phone. She came to Virginia in October of 1994 to visit. I took her to a Willie concert in Memphis where Willie came off the bus to meet us. I proposed to Helen after the concert, and we were married in January 1995, and have lived here with her sons, Jason and Rodney.

John and Sherry told me that Matthew had done this one last thing for me: he had given me a wonderful wife and two sons.
                        —Ree & Helen, Forest, Indiana

This isn't about anything changed in my life, it's what happened in the past. But the song I love is on the Alan Jackson cassette tape I have, "Home." I love it because it's a remembrance of my childhood. We were poor country folks back in the hills of West Virginia. Everything we ate was out of the garden. My mom canned everything she could get her hands on, because there were five brothers and one sister and me. My dad worked cutting timber. He didn't make much pay back then. We lived in an old house. They paid $6.00 a month rent, and he paid by the year, $72.00.

We had two pigs we butchered in the late fall of the year, so that was our meat. We made sausage and bacon, and we raised chickens, so we had eggs. Every once in a while, we'd have chicken on special occasions.

We didn't have electricity till I was 13. My mom washed clothes on the washboard every day, as we didn't get a washing machine until I was about 14. We burned oil lamps and Mom cooked on a wood stove. We had a pot belly stove in the front room for heat.

I had a good childhood with lots of love. We knew what "no" meant back then. We only got what we needed, not what we wanted. We got one pair of shoes a year for school. We lived way out in the country up a hollow. We went to a two-room school. My clothes were homemade.

When I hear Alan sing any song, it touches my heart, but "Home" is a special one of my childhood days.

—Helen, Hermitage, Pennsylvania

When I was a young girl, both of my folks were ill a lot and that meant long hospital stays for both of them. More than once they were both in the hospital at the same time, and as an only child, I was sent to live with relatives. Well, these people were kind to me, but not demonstrative in affection as my mom was. I usually cried myself to sleep every night I was there. I was insecure and scared. Of course, they eventually came home, and I had my parents again. That's when it started happening. I was about 13 at the time. Every time I'd leave home to go anywhere, I'd start to get "panic attacks." Panic attacks are a real illness. The symptoms are feeling sick to your stomach and dizzy with a rapid heartbeat, a cold sweat, and rapid breathing. I would get these attacks at school, overnight at a friend's house, or anywhere my folks weren't with me. Sometimes I'd get so sick I'd even have to go home from school.

I never dared go out to a game or a dance during my high school years, because I was afraid of getting sick. My illness continued as I went into my twenties. When I finally met the man that would be my husband, I never told him about my illness. I could go with him as long as we were in our city and as long as he didn't leave me alone. On our second anniversary, he tried to take me out of town on a vacation. I promptly got sick. I told him it was the "flu." From that time on until 1991, we seldom went anywhere. I had gotten a job, and because it was only five minutes away from home, I had managed to conquer my fears long enough to go to work each day. In fact, I threw myself into my job so I'd have an excuse "not to take" vacations. Then I got into country music.

The song that changed my life was "The River," written by Garth Brooks and Victoria Shaw. The song talks about living your dreams, not sitting on the shore line and saying you're satisfied: "Choose to chance the rapids and dare to dance the tide." Also, I love the line that says, "There's bound to be rough waters, and I know I'll take some falls, but with the good Lord as my captain, I can make it through them all." I had been a Christian almost all my life but had never trusted in the Lord as my captain to take care of my panic attacks. Then I made a decision. I shared my panic attack story with my Sunday school class, my close friends, and my husband, and asked for their prayers concerning my problem. And the first week in June, 1992, my husband and I went to Nashville. I took my "Ropin' the Wind" tape with me and played it all the way down there.

I waited in line at Fan Fair from 10 a.m. till 9:00 p.m. to get in to see Garth. We got within three feet of the door and they shut off the line. My husband said, "Well, honey, you tried." I told him, "If you think I drove 825 miles to go home without seeing Garth, you're crazy. I'm going to live my dream." So Wednesday night, with a second-degree sunburn from the day before, I slept on the cement by the gate of the Tennessee Fairgrounds. My pillow was my purse. On Thursday, I got in line to meet Garth again. And at 6:00 p.m. Thursday night, I got that hug I had driven 825 miles for. I got to live my dream, but the best part was to come. I have no more panic attacks. . . I'm free! I now love to travel. For the last four years we have come to Nashville. I spent over 30 years of my life in a "prison" of fear and lost so much. Now, I'm trying to "make up" for all that lost time.

For the rest of my life, whenever I get to go somewhere and do things I've never done before, I'll be thankful to the good Lord, and to Garth Brooks and Victoria Shaw for writing a song which changed my life forever: "The River."

—Chris, Sioux City, Iowa

A letter written to Doug Supernaw:

When I was pregnant with our second

child, our marriage crashed and burned. My husband moved out when our son was 10 months old and our daughter was six. It was a devastating experience for all of us. Bruce has been my true love, that kind of love you share only once—maybe twice if you're lucky and live long. It was a mutual decision, but I thought my heart would stop from the pain of it.

Your song, "I Don't Call Him Daddy", was a big hit while we were separated. It haunted me, followed me everywhere. I just could not stand the idea of Bruce having to wonder if his kids would ever call someone else Dad. I only saw your video once, but it cut through my heart. After two or three other signs from God, I made the decision that I would do whatever it took to make this marriage work.

I stopped the divorce proceedings and told Bruce that I could not go through with it. He said, "Well, you get no argument from me. I never wanted it!"

On December 8, 1994, we celebrated our

tenth wedding anniversary in grand style,
with new wedding rings, a night at the theat-
re, the whole bit. And I know that part of
this is due to God's hand and your music. It
pushed me over the line at a critical moment,
and it's affected the rest of my life.

—Alison, Evanston, Illinois

A letter written to Ricky Van Shelton:

Two years ago, I lost my precious wife,
Lorraine, after 53 years of wedded life, to
Alzheimer's disease. She used to go walking
with me at Texarkana Central Mall. They
had records and tapes. One day after we had
been up there, she said this tape on the TV
is mine. I said OK, but I never looked at it
then. But after she passed away, I looked at
it. It was your tape, "I'll Leave This World
Loving You." You can imagine how I felt.
Just a few days before she died, I went into
her room. As I was looking in on her, she

reached up and put her arm around my neck, and, pulling me down to her, she said these words: "I love you more than anything in this world." She never wanted to turn me loose. After she did leave me, I remembered the tape and I played, "I'll Leave This World Loving You."

I hope you know how I feel about the song. I shall never forget how I feel.

I am a country fiddler. I have played since I was nine years old and I am 76 now. Did you write this song? Whoever did knows how I feel.

Thanks for recording it. I will always know it was her song for me. May the Lord bless you and your lovely wife, Bettye, with many years.

—James, Roderea, Louisiana

A letter written to Aaron Tippin:

I love all of your work, but I especially

wanted to thank you for three songs that have really touched my life: "You've Got to Stand for Something," "I Wouldn't Have It Any Other Way," and "I Got It Honest."

My step-father came into my life when I was five and raised my two older sisters and me with as much love and kindness as any "real" father ever could have done. We were very poor when my mother married him. And though he couldn't afford it himself, he made sure we had everything we needed growing up. He was generous and thoughtful and he taught us to be proud of who we are. I simply can't say enough good things about him! He owns a small gas company (he and Mom are the only employees), and to this day works seven days a week and most nights, trying to pay off all the debt he acquired while raising us. My oldest sisters have gotten their college degrees, and I am a year away from getting mine. Only recently I've realized just how much I owe to this man who taught me so much about hard work, respect for others, and especially about love.

I don't get to go home much now, and when I do my father is either working his usual long hours or sleeping. He is getting up in years and his health is badly deteriorating. I know that my time left with my father is limited, but it's always been difficult for me to express my feelings. I could never put into words how much he's taught me about life! But, thanks to your songs, I've been able to do just that. I brought my tapes of yours home and played him those songs. I told him they reminded me of him. His true essence was captured in your songs, and I want to thank you for giving me the ability to "tell" my father all the things I never could before.

You've given me something very important—the chance to show my father that I love and admire him.

—April, Indian Trail, North Carolina

Years ago I knew this young man, since we were all going around in a gang, swimming, walking on the beach and fooling around as all young people do. He had a girlfriend, and I had a boyfriend. I didn't know he ever thought of me or ever loved me. So I married my boyfriend, and he married another girl after I got married.

Then World War II broke out and he came to my door with his uniform on as my husband was going to the store. He hugged me and said, "It should have been me." By then, I had a little girl and he had a little girl. We couldn't do anything about it.

After the war was over, he came to see me again. He wanted me to leave with him, but it wouldn't have been right to break up two families. I had to say no. But when Billy Ray sang, "It Should Have Been Me," it brought back all the memories. He went away and I have never seen him since. I heard rumors he is in a wheelchair, and others said he died. I'm a widow now, and I still love him as if it happened yesterday.

—Masie Edith, Canada

On September 3, 1992, at 6:00 a.m., six months into my pregnancy, I gave birth to a stillborn son. A routine ultrasound had revealed a gross heart abnormality inconsistent with life. Rather than carrying my dying baby to term, I had elected to have labor induced just 24 hours after receiving the devastating news. The stillbirth followed two previous miscarriages in 1990 and 1991.

Within days of leaving the hospital, while recuperating at home, I heard, for the first time, Billy Dean and Richard Leigh's "Somewhere in My Broken Heart." This exquisite song was painfully compelling. The song helped me access emotions which launched my lengthy grieving, and ultimately, healing process.

I believe this song exemplifies the universal power of music to touch the human soul. But "Somewhere in My Broken Heart" also had an unexpected personal impact. As with all of life's trials, some good things can result. The song led me to country music, and for the past three years, I have been exploring the historical and contemporary world of North America's finest musical tradition.

—Melanie, Kanata Ontario, Canada

My 37-year-old son, "Pratt," is mentally handicapped, and has been since an automobile accident at the age of six. He lives at home and is on medication.

In October of 1993, he very suddenly lost his father to a heart attack. It was harder on him than the rest of the family, and he was having a really hard time adjusting. He made friends with some neighbors. I thought it was great, until I realized he was becoming argumentative and even aggressive toward me. I came to realize he was smoking pot, and it was working against his medicine.

His father had always been there to guide

him and help control him when necessary. Since I could not control him by myself, I had to have him put in the mental hospital. I told him unless he admitted to smoking pot and did something to change, he would not be able to come home when he was released. It was Billy Ray Cyrus' influence that helped him turn his life around. He told me later, he kept wondering where he was going to live and then realized that was one of the songs Billy Ray had sung at the concert I took him to in Plant City, Florida.

Billy Ray made a lasting impression on him by the end of the first show. Pratt had gotten up near the stage and held his hand up in a peace sign, and Billy Ray had returned one to him.

He finally admitted to smoking pot and asked for help. He now goes to a mental health day program five days a week. He is working there two to three hours a day and getting paid for it. For Pratt, having to get up at 7:30 every morning to be somewhere on time is a major accomplishment. He is also planning on attending classes to get his GED.

I feel Billy Ray and his song "Where'm I Gonna Live When I Get Home" were the main influences on him. He is now coping with the death of his father and we are getting along really well.

—Shirley, Lady Lake, Florida

I got married to my high school sweetheart. Things were going good until my husband started drinking and taking drugs. He got me started and my life was a shambles. I was lying to everyone. I quit seeing my friends because of the abuse I was taking and getting from my husband. I filed for a divorce in January of 1992.

I moved in with my mom here in Missouri. But things got to me, so I found my own place, and I had my battles with alcohol and drugs. Well, one day I was at my mom's place for a few hours, I turned on my TV and there I saw Marty Stuart and Travis Tritt. I had no idea who they were until I saw them sing the song "The Whiskey Ain't Working No More." I fell to my knees and cried and thanked God for them, because I had been headed for destruction.

The song really hit me at home. I went back to my apartment and dumped out my bottles of Jack Daniels, and got the drugs and flushed them down the toilet. If it wasn't for Marty and Travis, I would either be in drug rehab or in jail or dead. I didn't like what I saw in the mirror, and I knew I had to change my life.

I have not been tempted to take a drink or do drugs, because I have an image of Marty and Travis with big frowns on their faces and their hands on their hips. I really feel that they would be very proud of me if they could see how much I have improved my life.

—Ronda, Marshall, Missouri

The song, "Coat of Many Colors," by Dolly Parton, has a special meaning for me. I had something similar happen to me when I was eight years old. And through Dolly's song, which I'm told was based on a true incident in her life, I came to realize that I wasn't the one who was inferior. The ones who were making fun of my clothes were the ones to feel sorry for.

My father walked out and left my mother in 1952 when I was four months old. I was the youngest of ten children, ranging in age from 21 years to four months. My father never came back, nor did he help us financially. My mother, who had always been just a farmer's wife, had to go to work at a local shrimp packing plant. Six years after he left, two of my brothers and two of my sisters were stricken with polio.

Needless to say, we were very poor. There were times when there was hardly enough to eat. Our clothes (usually hand-me-downs) were old, but they were always clean. The local church left bags of groceries at our door during the holidays.

Divorce was hardly heard of in our small town back in the 1950s. And so we felt different from most of the other children. Then, during the polio scare, people thought they might catch it from us—so that didn't help matters.

When I was eight and in the first grade, I had a sky blue blouse that was my favorite. Over a period of time, I lost the buttons one by one, and each time I did, I would find another button (any button) and sew it on myself. Eventually all the buttons were different and none really matched the blue blouse. One day I wore the blouse to school and a certain rich girl and her friends started laughing and teasing me about my blouse. I was crushed and completely humiliated. Over the years I never forgot that incident.

The first time I heard Dolly's song, "Coat of Many Colors," I cried for an eight-year-old girl who had been placed in a situation beyond her control. I also cried for the many children who, even now, through no fault of their own, are in similar circumstances. I know now that no one is inferior to anyone else. We are all the same, though some are more fortunate than others.

I will never forget Dolly's song. It still makes me cry.

I now have a beautiful home of my own. I drive the car I want, and buy the clothes I want. About a year ago, I was in a department store in Tampa that handles mostly designer clothing. While shopping, I came across an expensive dress. I fell in love with it and bought it. But the unusual thing about this dress is. . . all the buttons are different—different styles and colors. I had to laugh at the irony of it. I will always keep this dress. It reminds me of Dolly's song and of myself. And even though now I have pretty much anything I want, there will always be that eight-year-old girl inside me. No matter what I have or don't have, I will never mistreat anyone, nor will I stand by and see anyone mistreated in any way.

—Sally, Plant City, Florida

Letter written to George Jones:

I'm a 46-year-old guy, and Dad would've been 68 this year. Dad and I had a special relationship and were very close; but we were both stubborn as hell and wanted to be the toughest guy in town. We loved each other very much, but we were just too stubborn to tell each other how we felt. Simply saying "I love you" wasn't our style. We had to say it in our own way, and often it was hard to find the words. Dad was an electrician and I am a lineman. We're both hard-working, responsible men, and we both liked our whiskey and vodka. We may have drunk a lot, but we never missed a day's work because of it (although many days we didn't feel like working after our get-togethers the night before).

We both lived in Michigan. Dad decided to go to Texas this last winter. My wife and I received a phone call in February telling us that Dad's abdominal aorta had ruptured, and they didn't expect him to live. My wife and I started the long, icy, snowy drive from Michigan to Texas.

We arrived in Texas the next day to find that Dad had survived the surgery. With tears in our eyes, Dad and I held each other's hands. I still had trouble putting into words how I felt about Dad. Dad kept on improving, even though he remained on a respirator and his kidneys were failing. After seven days, we headed back to Michigan.

We continued to call the hospital twice a day to check on Dad's condition. He seemed to be slowly improving.

Dad's birthday was a week away. I told my wife to get a card for Dad. She told me it was too early to mail it, and I should wait for a couple of days until it was closer to his birthday. I told her I had to send it the next day. . . something told me I had to send it immediately.

My wife got the card and I was trying to think of how to put my love, respect, and admiration for my dad into words. I was sitting at home listening to your tape, "George Jones—Anniversary—Ten Years of Hits." Tears filled my eyes as each song seemed to remind me of my dad or our relationship. He was a whiskey-drinking, hard-fisted guy on the outside, but a big softie on the inside. He had grown up an orphan and learned at an early age to fend for himself.

The song, "Old King Kong," came on—and it instantly hit home. Even though the song was a love song between a man and a woman, the words expressed exactly what I felt for Dad. These were words that only Dad and I would understand. Dad grew up in an era when King Kong was the biggest and baddest there was. I took the birthday card and wrote these words to tell Dad how much I loved him: "Old King Kong was just a little monkey compared to my love for you." I insisted that my wife mail the card the next day.

Dad received the card two days before his birthday. He was still on the respirator and could not talk, but he was very alert and knew everything that was happening. The nurse read the card to Dad and showed it to him. As she read the part about Old King Kong, his eyes filled with tears and he looked at the nurse and gave her the "thumbs up" sign with his hand. The nurse told us this on the phone later that night when we called to check on Dad. I was so happy because I knew Dad understood my tremendous love for him.

We received a phone call the next morning telling us that Dad had passed away during the night. I was devastated to hear of the loss, especially since I had believed Dad was on the road to recovery.

I had no idea when I sent that card that those words about your song would be the last communication that I would ever have with my dad. You and your song made it

possible for me to let my dad know of my love. I am at peace knowing that Dad knew how I felt—and, at the very end, we had a special bond.

As the days passed after the funeral, I kept remembering the words of "Old King Kong," and their impact on me and my dad. These words had a special meaning that only Dad and I knew about. It became apparent to me that these were the words that had to be engraved on his tombstone. Most people question why I would have put something like that on a tombstone. They don't know that this was the last thing my dad heard from me, and that "thumbs up" sign he gave let me know he knew and understood.

—Lyn, Cass City, Michigan

Hi, I am 11 years old and my name is Kevin. I have a song "I Don't Even Know Your Name." I was traveling to a new place at a children's home. I was there one year. Then one day before I left I met this girl, a perfect one but 13 years old. She was watching me while I went off the high dive. I started walking her way. I said hi then swam off. Later on she grabbed my foot, but I swam off. But then she sent a girl over to ask if I will go with her. I said (yes)! I really liked her, but I did not know her

name. The next time I was at the pool I
found out what her name was. I got her
address and phone #. Her name is Regina. I
really like her. I dedicate "I Don't Even
Know Your Name" to her. And that is the
song that has a big impact on my life.

—Keven, Irving, Illinois